CAUGHT IN THE DARK

Dark Sons Motorcycle Club - Book Three

ANN JENSEN

Published by Blushing Books
An Imprint of
ABCD Graphics and Design, Inc.
A Virginia Corporation
977 Seminole Trail #233
Charlottesville, VA 22901

Ann Jensen
Caught in the Dark

eBook ISBN: 978-1-64563-941-1
Print ISBN: 978-1-64563-942-8
v1

Chapter 1

I'm not crazy, I prefer the term mentally hilarious.

A ngela was packing up her sexy secretary costume as a backup to her planned outfit for work. Her conservative but expensive bedroom was a distinct contradiction to the mass of sexy and naughty outfits she had laid out. The plan for tonight was a routine she had worked on all weekend, but options were always best when performing half naked for a room of unknown men.

Her neighbor Joshua flopped down on her bed with a dramatic sigh.

"Problems?" Angela held back a giggle as he sighed again. Her best and only friend loved drama and didn't know the meaning of boundaries. When she moved into the condo next to the flamboyant drag queen they had bonded over a shared love for technology and his/her sighs always meant trouble.

"Explain to me again why instead of spending tonight

clubbing with me you are taking your clothes off for ruffians to earn money you don't need?"

Joshua was a tall, beautiful man with buzzed black hair, a toned body and a complexion models would sell their firstborn to have. His cream Stella McCartney gown looked fabulous against his sepia skin tone but was a little too short for his long frame. His makeup and hair weren't done yet, which meant he stopped halfway into becoming Jojo to come talk to her. Angela liked him because from the first moment they met he ignored all of her many social inadequacies and just accepted her as she was. Well, mostly.

"Probably for the same reason a successful computer security specialist puts on a dress and killer heels twice a week and lip syncs for crowds of lusty gay men." She flopped down next to her friend and kicked up her bare feet.

"No, sugar. I am an attention whore who loves picking up young men. You, despite your porcelain skin and rocking purple hair, hate being in crowds, blush at the words big cock, and can't talk to a hot man long enough to lose your V-card."

Angela felt her cheeks heating and smacked her friend with a pillow. He was right, though she wouldn't admit it out loud. She had always been the brainiac, lost in books and her own thoughts. Raised by a workaholic single father, she had been a late life surprise which was more like a project to be managed than a child. When he died of a heart attack two years ago, it had been a wakeup call. One that said if she didn't want to die alone, something had to change.

"I love dancing. Becoming Cami on stage is my way of finding my wild side." She also loved losing herself in the sexy alter egos which came with stripping. She felt alive and powerful when she let her sexual side out to play.

"If you are looking for Mr. Right at a strip club, honey, someone done forgot to teach you some very basic facts about the types of men who frequent those places."

"Someone done? Is that your Princeton education showing though?"

"Don't get snooty with me, Harvard girl. At least they taught me men who like to shove cash in a girl's G-string aren't first time material."

"I'm not looking for the man for the first time, yet. I'm looking for what I want out of a first time." After her single disastrous failed attempt at a relationship when she was 19, she had given up. At 26, she had too many fantasies and until she decided which was right for her, how could she possibly pick a man? An equation with too many unknown variables just wasn't solvable.

"Honey, I am the last man on this planet to judge having an alter ego." Angela laughed because, Jojo, Joshua's drag queen persona, was the southern belle of any party while Joshua was as California as a black man could be. "But you know most of the women at that club offer more than just dances. And I don't want you to get hurt because some jerk mistakes you for one of them."

She did know that, and to be honest, it was one of the many reasons she picked Darklights to work at. Hearing about actual sex could only help her research. Besides, their security was amazing, both physical and digital – it had taken her several days to crack it – and she had watched months of videos confirming that not once was a girl there harmed. The few men who tried to step out of line had left with very expensive medical bills in their future.

In the four weeks she'd been working there, she hadn't felt pressured to do more than the two sets on stage and one private dance she agreed to. Angela even got to pick the customers she performed privately for from the requests and the bouncer always stayed in the room with her so there were no misunderstandings.

"I think it's sweet you worry."

Joshua gave an enormous sigh. "I guess I thought you would quit when I got you the internship at Vallier Technologies."

"Why would you think that?" Angela was excited to check out the new company that was on the cutting edge of every type of security.

"At the time, I thought it was odd that you lived here and were stripping. I assumed it was for the extra cash flow." Joshua rolled onto his stomach and gave her a hard look. "If you need more than they pay interns, I know I could get you a permanent position."

Angela laughed, rolling to hug Joshua. "I guess you never Googled me."

"No. Why? Do you have some scandalous videos out there?"

"Nothing like that!" She elbowed him and sat up. "Let's just say I'm good on money for the next 100+ years. I told you why I was dancing."

"I'm sorry, sweetie. I should have taken you at your word. You have to understand, a virgin computer geek stripping to find out what her inner slut wants, is a bit much. So why did you take the Vallier internship?"

Angela tried to put into words what was swirling in her head. She had done several internships, all at large tech companies, but by the time they offered her permanent employment she was bored. The idea of settling down and doing one thing for the rest of her life made her nauseous.

She had freelanced since she was 17 for the government and created and sold compatibility algorithms along with several other search and data mining programs. The profits from the sales had given her enough to live off the interest alone, even if she hadn't inherited millions from her father.

"I like what they do for kidnapped people and their work in encryption is fascinating. Besides, I checked, the morality standards and non-compete documents I signed don't preclude stripping as a side job. Actually, other than things that are illegal anyway, the company doesn't even have fraternization policies."

"Fine. You love me. I love you. Go get your freak on if that is really what makes you happy. I will just have to face my adoring fans alone, but only on Tuesdays and Thursdays."

Angela smiled at her drama queen of a friend. "You still want to carpool together tomorrow morning?"

"Of course! I can't wait to see you in that cute pantsuit we bought. So *'La Femme Nikita'*."

Although Vallier was a progressive company, Angela had decided to go more traditional for the first few weeks while she learned her way around. She loved her purple hair and crazy grunge style, but found people had a hard time taking her seriously. Maybe someday she would find the confidence to not care. Until then she would use clothes and hair like her favorite animal the chameleon did. Use them to blend into whatever identity she wanted to portray.

"And you can show the new girl around your technology empire."

"Oh, it isn't mine, but if Mr. Vallier even shows a hint of swinging that way, I will happily become the queen of his kingdom." Jojo struck a regal pose and she couldn't help but giggle.

"So not a scrawny geek?" Joshua liked his men on the big and buff side.

"You will get to meet him tomorrow he stops by every orientation. Then we can gossip about the unfairness of the genetic lottery he won on the drive home."

Angela laughed, picking up her duffle ready for a night of letting loose as someone else at the strip club.

Chapter 2

The best surprises are found in the strangest of places.

Tek was more than ready for a night, kicking back with his Dark Sons Brothers. Being the owner and CEO of Vallier Technologies meant he didn't get as much down time to spend with them as he would like. The work he did was important but that, along with his responsibilities to the Dark Sons Motorcycle Club, meant free time for fun was rare.

Darklights was one of the Motorcycle Club's semi-legitimate businesses. The semi part of the equation was that many of their very talented dancers offered extra services in the private rooms which might not conform to the current laws. Paying for a woman didn't appeal to Tek, but he understood why the simplicity of a transaction would tempt others. The plan tonight was to enjoy the scenery and head back to the Clubhouse and find a willing sweetbutt there to take the edge off.

He needed the fun tonight, since tomorrow he would be doing his least favorite part of being CEO—welcoming and answering questions for all the fresh-faced interns and new hires. He kept doing it because he believed it was important to meet every employee at least once, but their youth and optimism often made him feel old.

Several of his Brothers were sitting in the section reserved for Dark Sons and their guests. The women dancing in front of Puck and Grinder showed the party was already well under way.

Though they owned the place, the Dark Sons were completely different from most of the men here tonight. Most of the customers crowding the tables were well-dressed businessmen who on a Thursday night should probably be heading home to wives and kids but were instead here enjoying drinks and barely dressed women. The casual jeans, t-shirts, and leather cuts made them stand out, but no one dared say anything since they were a scary bunch of fuckers.

"Tek! Isn't this a school night for you?" Hawk joked. In his early fifties, the President of the Dark Sons MC had dark but graying military-short hair and a neatly trimmed beard. The gray hair was the only indication the man was getting older since he kept himself in peak physical condition.

"I'm surprised to see you here, old man. Isn't it past your bedtime?"

The two exchanged backslaps and sat. Highdive, the Sergeant at Arms for the Dark Sons, gave Tek a chin lift, but most of his Brothers were busy enjoying the show the two women were putting on in front of them.

"How goes saving the world?" Hawk took a drink and ignored the women, gyrating to the music and running their hands over each other's naked bodies. They were good looking, but Tek could tell this was a show. Let the younger men enjoy the fake stuff he preferred genuine passion.

"It goes, but it's feeling like I spend more time on the reports then on the important shit."

Vallier technologies was created to help people who were victims of kidnapping but had expanded to cover all forms of security. The pain of losing his four-year-old little sister when he was sixteen had driven him. First as a SERE instructor for the Rangers, then in building the company.

At thirty-three, he used his global contacts on both sides of the law to find those who couldn't protect themselves. With the help of his Brothers in Dark Sons, he had formed and made a success of a corporation which was half digital specialists and half highly trained mercenaries. So successful he now donated 25% of the company's services to law enforcement and private individuals who couldn't afford to pay.

Hawk gave an exaggerated shiver. "Death by paper-cuts. One of the many reasons I never want to go corporate."

A loud cheer filled the room. Tek looked around, trying to understand why the place was so packed.

"Hey Clean. What's with the crowd?"

The place was busy, like it was a Friday or Saturday night. Clean looked over and smiled. The Brother was average in everything. Height, weight, all of it was completely forgettable if you didn't know him well. His nickname had come from his ability to clean up messes and bodies so well cops wouldn't find a single trace. Manager of this strip club was his legitimate job, but every Brother knew his real talent was elsewhere.

"Got a new girl a month or two ago. She only works two shows two nights a week, but the white-collar crowd eats her up. Business has never been this good on a weeknight."

"She's that good?" Tek asked.

"Cami is fucking amazing," Puck shouted over the music.

"She's on next so you judge. Only does one private dance a night and we take a list of names that she picks from." Clean sat back in the booth to avoid getting a face full of ass as the girls had moved to pseudo-making out on the table.

"Seriously? Damn, the extras must be amazing if guys are signing up on a list." Tek was intrigued and couldn't wait to see if this woman was worth the hype.

One of the girls in front of him was gyrating like she was a man fucking her dance partner on the table. When the song stopped, the two girls popped up and the Brothers all slipped some money into their G-strings. The blonde smiled as Tek slipped a twenty in. He hadn't particularly liked the show, but the women had been energetic.

"Cami doesn't do extras," the girl practically purred. "But if you're interested, ask for Diamond and the executive package, I would love to accommodate you."

Tek gave the girl a small smile, not wanting to be rude as she slunk out of their section. No extras and a waiting list she controlled, he had to see this. All the girls except the servers walked to the back as the club lights dimmed and the MC came over the speakers.

"Now it's time for one of Darklights' newest performers." The crowd let out cheers and whistles. "Like the chameleon, she's named after, every week she shows us a new color. We've met the wild girl, the mistress, the cowgirl, and the punk. Tonight, I think you will all be happy to meet little girl Cami."

Tek wanted to laugh at the dirty ideas that flitted through his mind as the announcer rattled off her unique acts. His chuckle cut off as Cami appeared and actually skipped onto the stage. Her vibrant purple hair was up in two pigtails which brushed her shoulders. She was wearing a white, little sundress that barely covered her ass with pink pearl snaps down the front. She was maybe 5'9" in the platform, white Mary-Jane style heels which had to be 5" of her height.

It wasn't her looks which caught him, though her tits and ass were absolutely perfect, it was the joy in her eyes. She skipped around the stage at first, bending and waving to the audience as if she was a little girl greeting old friends. Each bend gave those in front of her a perfect view down her dress to the gorgeous cleavage and those behind a tempting view of perfect globes lightly hugged by white cotton.

A light pop song came on and she squealed jumping up and down the movement undoing the top two snaps and giving a glimpse of white lace. Transfixed, Tek watched as she swung with childlike abandon around the stripper poles slowly giving bigger glimpses of what was under the dress. It was so wrong it was right and made him remember watching girls on the playground when they would inadvertently flash the overeager boys.

The next song rolled in with a slightly darker beat and his breath hitched as she threw herself at the pole and spun until somehow, she was upside down. Her dress slipped to the floor revealing the sheer white lace panties and bra he had wanted to see for the last few minutes. Her golden skin showed no tan marks and the underwear, unfortunately, had just enough fabric he couldn't see the color of her nipples or if she shaved completely.

With a gasp she pulled herself upright, color lighting her cheeks with embarrassment as she clutched the pole, staring down at her wayward clothing, as if shocked her clothing had slipped off. He wanted to run up on stage and cover her, wanting the sight of her beauty all to himself. A pulsing beat filled the music, and she dropped a bit, gasping as the pole rubbed her between her legs and he watched as her breath started a panting rhythm in time with the music. The crowd cheered, and she bit her lip and slowly started pulsing against the pole, each movement sending shudders across her muscles.

It was like watching a girl find her first sexuality played out on stage. Though Tek's mind told him she was in her early twenties and this was a show, they paid her to do, his body wanted more than anything to get up there and help her discover the pleasure her body could produce.

The look of surprise on her face as she gyrated and twisted her own nipples through her bra made his dick so hard, he was afraid the zipper was going to leave permanent marks. She never stopped dancing, but somehow each movement took him on a journey. Men threw money at the stage and she didn't even seem to notice, but she would always end up on the side of the stage where the most money lay like a carpet of green.

The last song was a deep dark rhythmic number. She alternated doing moves on the pole which made him want to take its place and floor work that had him convinced she was masturbating right in front of them all. Lust poured through his veins and played hell with his usual control. He felt himself wishing the VIP booths weren't lit like the floor so he could adjust himself without his Brothers noticing.

Cami had her back to the pole and her hand was down her panties making circles to the beat while her other arm gripped the pole above her head. She looked over and Tek felt their gazes lock. His breath matched hers as she started thrusting. He swore if he could break the gaze he would see her fingers disappearing inside her sweet cunt.

As the song came to an end, her face relaxed and she threw her head back in ecstasy, breaking their gaze for a moment. When her muscles stopped twitching, she looked back at him as her hand slid out of her panties and her fingers glistened. As she lifted the fingers to her mouth, the lights dropped, and the room was silent. Cheers and screams for more burst through the room and Tek dropped back into his seat, more sexually aroused than he had been in years. Or ever.

Dim lights came up and two of the servers were cleaning the money from the stage into metal buckets.

"Damn." Tek grabbed a beer from the bucket and took a long drink.

Hawk adjusted himself in his jeans, and grabbed a beer for himself. "Christ, Clean, that girl needs a warning label or something."

"You should see her with a corset and a whip." Clean laughed. "But that one is a bag of issues with 'keep away' written all over it."

Tek couldn't imagine the issues which would make any man hesitate getting closer. "Drugs?"

"No, the girls are screened weekly for that and STDs. The girl you saw on stage doesn't exist. The second she is not performing; she is a completely different person. That other person isn't all there upstairs."

"That was Cami, everyone! Remember, there are only ten more minutes to sign up for a chance of a private dance from her. We will announce the lucky winner in forty minutes." Three different women strutted out onto the stage and began their version of entertainment.

Tek only had one more question for Clean. "How do I get on the list?"

Chapter 3

Eenie, Meenie, Miney… Oh yeah.

ngela sat in the dressing room trying to pull herself together. She pretended to orgasm on stage occasionally. Sometimes more than once during a set, but this was the first time she had actually done it for real. The presence of the man with an intense gaze at the owner's table had pushed her on from the moment she noticed him when she first came out.

The whole time she danced, she could feel his gaze on her like velvet heat. She had pictured him as her bad boy neighbor watching her through his window. It fed the fantasy and made her performance almost too real. When he caught her gaze near the end, she knew he wanted to see her come while he watched. And she had!

Cami was supposed to be outside of Angela, only skin deep. A way to try wild and wicked things without touching the person she was at her core. But tonight, it had felt like it was Angela on stage and with the blond mystery man watching. She had loved it. Did it mean this experiment in her sexuality was working or had gone too far?

"Seriously hot show tonight, Cami." Karen, one of the club's waitresses, carried in her bucket that held her tips. Angela didn't like the tipping part of dancing but knew it would be too strange to refuse. So, she had made a deal with the waitresses on her first night. If they cleaned up the money after her set, they could keep ten percent. She didn't really care if they took more. Stripping was an odd job. You paid the house a fee for every dance you did, like renting time on stage. Tips were your actual pay, so anything left after covering the fee was yours to keep. Since she didn't need the money, if there was anything left after covering house costs, she donated it to her favorite women's charity.

"Where do you want your tips?"

"I'll t-take them." Her damn stutter always hit when she was uncomfortable. Looking down, she saw she had done really well on both of her sets tonight. She'd already tipped out everyone and paid her house fees for the night out of her first dance set and had almost three hundred left. She shoved the money into the cloth bag in her locker for just that purpose.

"Why don't you do more sets or more nights? You could be rolling in it." Karen seemed truly puzzled. The woman worked shifts both as a waitress and as a dancer while putting herself through school.

Angela shrugged. "The club minimum is t-two stage s-sets and one set off stage." Ugh, she even stuttered quoting rules. She sounded stupid.

"So, you literally do the minimum?"

"Yup." She blushed and looked down at her hands, not wanting to say more.

Jasmine, another of the club's dancers, ran into the room,

a jumbled mess tossing off her shoes and ripping open her locker. "Shit shit shit!"

Angela had never seen the woman so flustered. "What's wrong?"

The woman was pulling her street clothes on. "My kid's running a 104 temp and throwing up like the exorcist. I got to pick her up and take her to the emergency room." She slammed her locker door, frustrated tears making her eyes sparkle. "Not that I have any clue how I'm going to pay for that and rent this month." She pulled her top on and slammed her fist into the locker. The tears began to run down her face, leaving trails of mascara over her made up cheeks.

Angela stood and pulled the woman into a hug. She hated that people struggled with the things which should be basic in life. Jasmine let out a sob and relaxed against her for a moment. After a few breaths, the woman drew away, pulling herself together.

"Here." Angela grabbed the bag of money from her own locker. "If you need more, just let me know."

"I can't take your money, Cami," Jasmine said, but really looked like she wanted to.

"Consider it a loan if you have to."

"Really?" The hope in her voice hurt Angela's heart.

"Yeah. And I'm serious if you need more, let me know." The woman hugged her so hard she thought she heard bones creaking. Jasmine shoved the cash in her purse and took off as one of the bouncers, oddly named Decaf, came back and handed Angela the list of names she had to choose from.

"Great show tonight, Cami." He gave her and Karen a nod and headed back into the club.

"You are too good for this place," Karen teased.

"You just say that because I tip out well." Her voice was so quiet Karen probably didn't hear her. If these girls knew how little she needed the money, she knew they would consider her an even bigger freak. Angela looked over the list, always hating this part of the night. She usually used a formula which divided the time she received the list by the month/day and rounded down. She used the resulting number to count through the list, alternating counting the VIPs or non-VIPs twice. It made the choice as random as her mind could handle. Private dances were harder for her to stay in character and after her experience on stage tonight she wasn't sure if she could do a good job.

"Holy Shit! It looks like you have a bunch of Dark Sons on your list tonight." Karen leaned over her shoulder, staring at the paper.

The Dark Sons Motorcycle Club owned Darklights and there were always a few of them around either working or enjoying the shows. The other girls who worked here raved about what good tippers they were. A lot of the women partied with the club outside of work and if the stories were true, these men were wild and only loyal to their Brothers.

At the bottom of her list were several bolded names which she guessed were the Brothers since she doubted any of the usual VIPs had names like Grinder, Hawk, or Tek.

"D-do you know any of them?" Cami handed Karen the list, having already memorized it.

"Yeah, let's see. Hawk is their President, hard body, scary eyes. Puck is the cute Ken doll looking guy, well if Ken rode a Harley. Grinder's nice but handsy." That put him out of her running. "Highdive is the Sergeant at Arms, he scares me, but in a good way. Tek is the Secretary. I haven't seen him around much, but he's supposed to be a computer genius or something." Karen bit her lip. "Pick Hawk. I mean, he is their President."

Angela thought about it and Karen was probably right, but she kinda liked the idea of the smart tough guy. She was going to look down at her watch to start the math to pick, but then she remembered the outfit she had planned for next week. It was in her locker, almost like fate had told her to bring it. Maybe tonight she would forgo the random calculation and pretend she believed in destiny.

"I think I'm going to play naughty secretary for the Secretary."

Karen laughed. "Damn girl, you will have him panting."

She hoped she had chosen right.

―――――――――

The dancers on stage held no interest for Tek after seeing Cami dance. It had never occurred to him before that most dancers had blank almost dead looks in their eyes, like their bodies might be performing athletic and sexy movements but their minds were elsewhere. It amazed him that many of the men here didn't care or even seem to notice.

"Haven't seen much of you lately. Anything I need to know about?" Hawk leaned forward, taking a sip from his beer.

Tek rubbed his eyes, feeling some of the stress of the last year pull down on him, and sighed. "Nothing that affects the club. Just some crap with the company. We expanded so much last year, I lost touch with everything that was going on. We won a big government contract on the digital side that is supposed to go live in a month, but I'm seeing odd anomalies on the corporate clients who we are using as guinea pigs to test it out."

"Anything we can help with?"

Hawk's offer reminded Tek of why he would always be loyal to the Dark Sons. They were his family and would have his back no matter what.

"No. Just needed some time away from the problem. Fuck,

I never thought I'd be stuck in an office eighty hours a week, but that is what my life has become."

"Then quit."

Hawk's words hit him like a punch to the gut. It wasn't like he hadn't thought about it before but hearing it from his Brother made it feel like an actual possibility.

Hawk looked him up and down. "Seriously, Brother. You used to love what you do. Hell, if it wasn't for your skills, we couldn't do half the shit we do, but when do you get to live? Do you need a second billion in your bank account? If you don't enjoy life, what is the point?"

What was the point? He had started Vallier Technologies as a way to help victims of kidnapping and violence. The last few years it had grown more into a tool for corporations to protect their bottom line. They still did good, but his time was taken up by the nonsense. Maybe it was time to think about selling off the parts he didn't care about.

"You make it sound easy." Tek shook his head.

Hawk smiled and leaned back in the booth. "Nothing worth having is easy, but it can be simple."

Tek finished his third beer as he took in his President's words. The song playing stopped and the MC's voice came over the speakers, "I hope you are all enjoying the wonderful delights we have to offer here at Darklights. Before our next dancers take the stage, I have the pleasure to announce tonight's lucky winner of a private dance with Cami is Tek!"

Decaf, one of the Club's Prospects, laughed from behind him. "Damn, I was sure she would pick Hawk."

"You put my name on the list, Prospect?" Hawk scowled.

Clean slapped their President on the arm as the Prospect went pale. "No. I put everyone's name down. Her dances are life changing even if she doesn't lay a finger on you."

Hawk only looked a little less pissed as he slugged Clean in the arm. "I don't need pay-to-play pussy."

Tek raised an eyebrow. "And I do?"

Hawk smirked. "With that pretty boy hair and the desk job making you soft, I guess you gotta do what you have to to get the sweet stuff."

Tek flipped off his President and turned to the Prospect who had regained a little of his color to show him the way. The private room had a leather couch and just enough room for dancing or fucking, depending on your point of view. It wasn't his first time in a private room, though it had been a few years. This woman sparked something in him, and he was eager for more.

Even picking up women at the Clubhouse had become routine. Find a hot chick, foreplay till she came, fuck till they both came, and take off before she became clingy. He couldn't remember the last time he even wondered what one of his partners was like outside the bedroom.

Something about this woman had his imagination going wild. Did she fantasize about the things she played out on stage? Roleplaying was his secret kink. He'd tried with a few partners, but it had never progressed beyond a little dirty talk. He sat, trying to hide his impatience from Decaf, who leaned against the wall by the door.

Tek was annoyed that the Prospect looked like he was going to be staying in the room. He wanted alone time to pick apart the mystery which was Cami. With a temptation like her, the extra layer of security was probably needed with her regular customers.

The door swung outward and a vision of painful temptation stood backlighted. Her hair was done up in a tidy bun. Adorable little glasses were perched on the tip of her cute nose. She wore a black pencil skirt with a slit which let him get a glimpse of the edge of thigh-high stockings. It showed off gorgeous legs in five-inch black stiletto heels. Her suit jacket was buttoned up to the bottom of lush cleavage and he didn't think she had a blouse on. She held a pad of paper and a pen in her hands like she was ready to take notes.

He wasn't sure what he expected, but Cami in this sexy suit had him speechless. Her prim expression broke for a minute as she caught sight of Tek, and nervousness flashed in her eyes. Her chest shuddered as she took a deep breath. Eyes now sparkling, she stepped in the room, her lips thinned in a serious expression, and she turned to the Prospect.

"Thank you, Mr. Decaf, you can wait outside by the door."

Chapter 4

The only difference between a good girl and a bad girl... is good girls are selective with who they are bad with.

Angela did her best not to blush at Decaf's wide eyes as he left the room. Tek's magnetism had her pinned in place. Up close, he was even more devastating to her libido. Powerful tattooed arms crossed over a well-muscled chest unfortunately covered by a plain black t-shirt. His Dark Sons leather vest added to his aura of danger and his perfectly styled dirty blond hair just beckoned her to mess it up. She licked her dry lips, trying to focus.

Telling the bouncer to leave had been a crazy impulse. One she hoped she didn't regret. Truth was wanted nothing to ruin the fantasy with this man. They might only have fifteen minutes, but she was determined to enjoy each second. She wouldn't break her rules of no touching but knew tonight she would do just about anything else for this man who seemed to have a direct connection to her libido.

She let herself fall into the role she had chosen and put on her best professional voice. "My rules for our time are very s-simple and few. You may not touch me. I will not t-touch you. How would you like to proceed Mr. Tek?"

His eyes drew a long slow fiery line down her body, caressing every inch of her like warm fingers down her skin. "Well, Ms. Cami, I accept your rules, though I can say I'm disappointed. I think you are missing out on the benefits of what I could do for you."

Her core grew wet. His voice was as professional as her own, sending thrills at the thought that someone was going to play along with her silly games for once.

"Would you like music? It's my first day as your secretary, so you will have to instruct me on what to do. I've never worked for such a powerful man before."

He tapped the music controls and soft sultry music played. Tek stood and her pulse raced as he moved closer. Her breath quickened as he got so close, she could feel the heat from his body, but nothing else. He bent slowly, his breath tickled her ear as he growled, "Is that what you like, power? Why didn't you pick Hawk then?"

She shivered. He didn't seem angry, but his fierceness demanded an honest answer. Her voice was barely a gasp when she answered, "I thought a secretary for the Secretary would be fun."

He moved slightly, his eyes catching hers and his breath warm against her lips. "No other reason?"

She wanted to break her own rules and lean forward and kiss him but restrained herself, barely. "No." Her answer was more a whimper than words.

Deft fingers plucked her glasses off her face without even a brush against her skin. Then he took the pad and pencil out of her shaking hands and tossed them on the couch. When he stepped back, she swayed slightly, missing the warmth of his body. Tek sat back down on the couch, looking like a king on his throne.

"I need my secretary to be able to take direction, have a good memory, and know what pleases me. Do you think you handle that, Ms. Cami?"

"I'll try, Sir."

His small smile sent goosebumps up her arms. "Take off the jacket."

"Is that appropriate, Sir?" Cami blushed hoping he would play along with her and not get annoyed that a stripper was balking at getting undressed.

He clicked his tongue as if in disappointment. "Already questioning direction." He shook his head. "You look hot. I want you to be comfortable."

"Sorry, Sir."

Her fingers trembled as they slowly undid the three buttons. Her excitement grew as she realized he would play her game. The emerald green bra she wore was sheer, and she loved the contrast against her pale skin. Nervous he might not like it as much as she did, she clutched the jacket in front of her after giving him a peek at what was underneath.

"Fold the jacket and place it nicely on the chair."

Needing to please him and feeling the music pulsing through the room she swayed her hips slowly as she followed his instructions. The hunger that filled his eyes made her feel powerful. It took a lot of work to keep her curvy body from slipping into overly lush given her sedentary lifestyle. By the standards of the shallow, she was considered overweight. They could jump off a cliff for all she cared, she wouldn't starve herself. The heat in his eyes said clearly, he wasn't one of those shallow men.

"Turn around, run your hands down your sides, then slip off your skirt and let me admire your beautiful ass."

"Sir?" She tried for outrage but her desire filled her voice.

"You must not have a good memory if three instructions are too complicated." He leaned forward with a smile. "I thought you wanted this job, but obviously pleasing me is not your first priority. I guess I'll have to find someone else."

"No, Mr. Tek I need this job!" Her nipples tightened at how wonderfully he was feeding her fantasy.

He raised an eyebrow and leaned back. "Prove it."

She turned, his tone of command spoke to a need inside her she had never known existed. With only words he had her more worked up than she had ever been before. Maybe that was what she needed, a dominant partner. Her one boyfriend had been so passive they had never even kissed unless she initiated it. Nothing like this sexy, rough biker.

She ran her hands down her sides and shivered as she imagined they were his hands. She unzipped the material and let it drop to the ground. She bent and made the movement as sexy as she could. Her long hair fell out of the tight bun she had put it up in and her purple hair swept down against her legs. She knew her ass was perfectly on display to him sitting there, the matching emerald thong barely even covering her pussy.

"Like this, Sir?"

"Very good. Are you wet for me, naughty girl?"

"I'm sorry, Sir." Angela's voice was husky with arousal.

"That makes me very happy." The deep timber of his voice filled the space. "Turn around and display your breasts."

Angela didn't usually do topless but she had already pushed him and didn't want to disappoint him again. She stood up and turned. Shyly she scooped her breasts out of the cups of her bra, leaving them supported but on display to his hungry gaze.

"Play with your nipples." His gaze got sleepy. "I hate your rules right now, I want to be sucking on those pretty tits listening to you moan as I nibble and lick each one until you are so wet your honey is dripping down your thighs."

Angela moaned. She pinched lightly at first, then moaned as she twisted each nipple in turn. It wasn't hard to imagine his grip, and she tightened more, knowing he wouldn't be gentle with her. Lightning shot straight to her clit and her inner walls trembled as if on the verge of orgasm.

"Take your panties off and give them to me."

Glad she had put the underwear on over her garter belt, she slipped them down quickly. Air hit Angela's wet pussy, and she wondered if he liked the fact she had gotten a full wax a few days ago. The silken material landed in his hand and she held her breath, waiting for his next command.

"Come closer, I want to see my secretary's pretty pussy up close."

Tek's dirty talk excited and embarrassed her. She had never had a man gaze at her most private part so closely before. The thought that he wanted to, made her excitement ratchet up even further. She stepped and positioned herself between his legs. They were technically touching, but she didn't care anymore.

"You smell like heaven. I can almost taste you on my tongue. Lie down on the couch and spread for me. I want to watch you make yourself come."

She lay down beside him on the couch, heat burning her cheeks, and propped one leg up behind his head, putting herself on full display. With one hand she spread her pussy lips, while she used the fingers of the other to slowly circle her clit.

"Fuck. Your clit is so hard I can see it begging for attention. Pinch it for me, sweetheart. Know that I want to be tongue deep inside you eating up your sweet honey. Damn, I can see it dripping down your ass."

Light flickered behind her eyelids and she moaned loudly as she followed his directions.

She felt so empty inside and had to slip fingers inside her opening to relieve just a little of the ache.

"Look at me while you fuck yourself. I want you imagining how much better it would be if it was my cock filling and stretching your tight little cunt."

She locked eyes with his gray gaze and was lost. She wanted it to be his cock filling her. So much for not finding a man she wanted at a strip club. She wanted him to consume her. Shut down every whirling thought in her mind and replace it with pleasure. She was about to tell him that when her orgasm blindsided her.

"Tek!"

Tek watched Cami thrash as her orgasm overtook her. The purple of her hair, a beautiful contrast against the cream of her skin and the black leather of the couch. His cock ached to slam into the pink folds which were so tempting and close. He knew if he pushed her, she wouldn't stop him, but some instinct warned if he acted on the impulse, he would never get to spend time with her again.

He wanted hours with her, and he didn't want it to be in the back room at a strip club with a timer counting down the minutes. Decaf had popped his head in a minute or two earlier, probably intending to say his time was up. When he had taken in the scene, he had wisely ducked back outside, saying nothing. Tek didn't think Cami had even noticed.

He needed to get her back in clothes or there was no way his self-restraint was going to last. "That was gorgeous, and I would love to see it again, but our time is up."

Cami looked around, confused, then seemed to pull herself together. He couldn't hold in the laugh as she almost kicked him in the head in her haste to sit up.

"Sorry! So, s-sorry." She grabbed at her jacket, buttoning it up crooked in her haste to cover up.

Where had the sleek coordinated seductress gone? Tek found he liked this awkward, shy version of her almost as much. The tiny stutter, which gave away her nerves, was adorable. When she started to put her skirt on inside out, he decided she needed some guidance.

"Cami, eyes on me." He made sure his voice was low and commanding.

Within moments her body relaxed, and he wanted to growl in pleasure. Tek had thought he had noticed submissive signals from her but had thought it part of her act. Tek required control in almost every aspect of his life, but he especially liked it in the bedroom. This woman was becoming more and more appealing to him.

"Slowly and sexily redress yourself."

A playful smile flashed over her face and she became the graceful temptress from earlier. She redressed everything perfectly, but when she reached for her panties, he smiled and pocketed them.

"Much better," Tek said, then decided to push his luck. "I would like to see you again."

Her cool mask faltered, and she looked lost again. "I dance again on Th-Thursday night."

He was disappointed she didn't seem ready to see him except in a professional capacity and doubted any offer he might make would be welcome at this point. He hadn't made it as far as he had in life by giving up on things he wanted.

"I guess I'll just have to wait till then." They would be two long days.

She was a wonderful, sexy mystery he wanted to unravel but for right now he would step back. He would come Thursday, but if she didn't pick his name off the list for her private time, this little chameleon would find out just how persuasive he could be in getting his way.

Chapter 5

I'm not antisocial. I'm just not user friendly.

ngela stood in front of her mirror on the verge of tears. Her two wigs taunted her with an impossible decision. Blonde and people would think she was fun and vibrant. Black and she would be the mysterious new girl. Thank God, Joshua had picked out her clothes. The Versace suit along with the chunky silver necklace and leather belt were perfect for either choice. The pantsuit screamed elegant professional and might help distract people from her nerves. She had braided and pinned her purple hair close to her head but was paralyzed in deciding between the blonde or black hair.

New things sucked. Options had to be evaluated, or how could she be sure she made the right choice. Visualizing all possible outcomes was part of her process. Why had she agreed to work again? Her last internship had ended when her boss had suggested she fill out disability paperwork so they could accommodate her special needs. Mortifying!

He thought she was autistic. She wasn't. Several psychologists who administered batteries of tests agreed. Severe social anxiety was the preferred diagnosis. Panic attacks and nonstandard reaction to stress made people uncomfortable around her. The stuttering and quoting of relevant facts when nervous didn't help.

When she refused medication, her last psychiatrist had suggested playacting as a coping mechanism. Pretend to be someone else until she knew how to feel about a situation. Then when ready she could be herself again. So far it worked. Though she doubted he had intended for her to become a stripper to find her sexual identity.

"Your chariot awaits, beautiful." Joshua's sing-song voice came from her living room.

Angela jumped. Panicked, she looked at her bedside clock. She had lost almost an hour debating over her hair choice. There was no time for breakfast. She dropped her head in defeat. The idea of working for Vallier Technologies was exciting. The research into facial recognition software exhilarating. The ideas she had come up with on how to create a search algorithm that would start working on probable data sources first to reduce the time needed to go through video feeds for kidnap victims could be groundbreaking.

Why would they want someone as indecisive as her working for such a wonderful company? Now that she didn't have time to eat, she might pass out. If she did that, her coworkers would lose confidence in her ability to function. Without social support within the office, she would again have to work alone. If she worked alone, she would overwork to compensate. Without free time, she would lose her only friend because she wouldn't have time to—

"Oh no, you have that look." Joshua cut off the spiral of her thoughts as he stepped into the room.

Angela held out the wigs with a wordless plea. He looked each over, shaking his head.

"I don't know why you don't just stick with the purple. I promise no one would care."

"It's not professional and you never get a second chance to make a first impression." Her father had taught her that, and it was one of life's great truths. It took a long time to fix a bad first impression, and by then it was usually too late.

"Black dear. You don't have a tan and the blonde will wash you out."

Angela kissed him on the cheek and took five minutes to be sure it was pinned tight to her head and looked natural.

"Ready?" Joshua handed her a banana nut muffin, proving to her once again why he was the best friend in the world.

The Vallier office complex was so beautiful. Four stories of glass and chrome in the middle of a gorgeous landscape. How did any of the employees resist the urge to sit outside all day and take in the mountain view? The security at the location was impressive, with friendly guards at the front gate and sitting inside the principal building.

Joshua led her inside the pristine white building and helped her get her temporary security badge. Anxiety was an all too familiar feeling building in the back of her mind as he walked her among the low cubicles which housed people already hard at work.

"Relax, honeybunch. I can hear your teeth grinding." Joshua rubbed her shoulder in what was probably supposed to be a comforting gesture.

"This was a mistake. I'm going to just e-mail research and

development with my ideas and offer to work as a consultant from home." Angela stopped walking and turned to leave. Being an intern was silly. She had done it three times before, and she never lasted more than a few months. The need to please supervisors and meet new people was overwhelming.

"Angela." Joshua quickly stepped in front of her and blocked her retreat. "You can't keep hiding from the world."

"I'm not hiding. I'm being strategic with my productivity. Socializing can take between twenty to fifty percent of the average worker's day. Add onto that the commute time and two to five hours of my day, which could be spent on designing and optimizing programs, is wasted."

"And you end up a friendless, shut-in, virgin without even pets to keep you company."

"I have friends."

"Other than me, name one person you talk to on a regular basis who knows your real name." Joshua's raised eyebrow was like an accusation.

So maybe he was right. Strippers and hackers didn't exactly make for close companions when you were hiding your identity from them. Angela dropped her head, letting the straight black hair of her wig cover her face. The probability that this internship would end in social embarrassment was pretty high, but if she didn't try, nothing would ever change.

"Honey, if you can take your clothes off to find your sexual self, you can sit in an office and find your social self."

She wanted to be normal. Or at least her own version of that word. She wanted to find people who would accept her and all her quirks without pity or condescension. The only way to do that was to put herself out there like she was doing at Darklights.

"Fine. I calculate only a 22% chance of this ending in anything but disaster. But fine." She took a deep breath. "I will try."

"Good, because here comes your new supervisor." Joshua raised his voice a bit. "Rick, this is your new intern, Angela."

Angela looked up, her pulse racing. The man walking towards them could have stepped out of the pages of middle-management monthly. Dark brown hair gelled into the latest style, his white button-down shirt looked freshly starched, and his red satin tie was perfectly centered. He looked so unlike a programmer she had to do a quick re-evaluation. Rick reminded her more of a slick salesman than someone who led a department that focused on digital security.

Hopefully, something was going wrong in his day because if an expression of annoyance was his default state, she didn't have much hope for a fun, open, working environment. She straightened her shoulders and offered her hand to him.

"I'm looking forward to working on your team."

Rick shook her hand and gave her a once over that reminded her a little too much of the hungry glares men often gave her on stage. "Aren't you a little old to still be in college?"

Angela wanted to kick the smug man right where it counted to remind him of his manners. Stats of average college age graduation as well as the thousands of reasons one might want to start as an intern even when not a student flooded her thoughts. Twenty-six was not old considering she earned her first degree at sixteen. She was going to lay into him, but Joshua stole her thunder.

"Actually, Angela has two doctorates and just defended a third."

She was currently under review for two more doctorates at Cambridge and the University of Colorado. It wasn't worth interjecting the information since those would be honorary based on the research she had done for the universities instead of time spent in classes. Research was relaxing and had given her something to fill her time while coming to terms with her father's death. The classes to earn the first two had been boring, but her father had insisted she wouldn't be taken seriously without them.

"Well, I guess the job market is slim for some people. Good for you, working with what you can get. I'll show you your workspace." Luckily, Rick turned and sauntered away, or he would have seen the furious expression on his newest employee's face.

"Be good, girlfriend. Brawling on the first day is discouraged." Joshua's playful grin as he whispered soothed her nerves a bit.

"I was thinking a Hello Kittie porn virus to his personal email, but I will hold off for now." She rubbed her sweaty palms on her hips. "I'll see you, Joshua."

Angela followed as far behind her new boss as she reasonably could, biting her tongue the whole way.

Chapter 6

Surprises are only fun with presents and parties.

Tek studied the troubling reports on his desk with a scowl. Two of the companies they provided security for were reporting possible breaches on the electronic front. The fact they both used Vallier's premier services should make hacking close to impossible, but the evidence was piling up. He continued to keep his hands in certain projects, but the company had grown so much over the last few years it was hard to keep up. Maybe Hawk was right, and he should consider turning this stuff over to someone younger with more enthusiasm.

He hated it, but for now he would need to clock in overtime to personally look into things. Just the thought made him tired. What he needed was a vacation, some downtime to get his creative-self working again. A distraction like the purple haired goddess from last night would be perfect.

Those soft curves and playful yet submissive blue eyes

would remind him there was more to life than just work and the Dark Sons. Getting the little stripper's information from the Darklights' computers would be the work of moments. Planning out his seduction of her would be stimulating.

The way she had morphed from a schoolgirl into sexy secretary had been fascinating, to say the least. One of the reasons he had never settled for just one woman was how little time it took before he was bored. His quick mind and out of the box thinking had made his company such a success, but if it hadn't been for the important work they did on missing people, he would have long ago sold out and started something new.

This woman was perfect for some kinky roleplaying. She would hold his interest for more than the usual hour. He had already come up with several fantasies that had her right at their center. Would she take requests?

"You busy, Boss?" Kane's voice called from his open door.

Kane was the head of the mercenary arm of Vallier Technologies and a longtime friend. His almost black hair and intense stare had most people too afraid to approach. Tek had been his SERE instructor back in the day, and the man was one of the few who had graduated the program with perfect marks. So, when Tek had expanded from digital to physical security, he had sought out and gotten the best and most honorable ex-military men he could find and paid them what they were worth.

"Come on in. I'm just looking over some problems from the technology side."

Kane came in and shut the door behind him. At thirty-six, the man was still in prime shape and often led the most dangerous missions himself. The look on his face told Tek his day wasn't about to get easier.

"I thought you would be busy prepping your fresh meat

speech. Practicing your speech to calm the little geeks down, so they can grow up to be nice little drones for your empire."

Tek snorted. "Yes, you know how much I love the rah-rah. Something important must be brewing for you to be in here instead of out there showing off your muscles hoping the new coeds will fall on your dick."

"Have I thanked you enough for not having a 'no fraternization' policy?" Kane sat down in the chair in front of his desk.

"Since I don't think there is a young single desirable woman at my company you haven't fucked, you really should be sending me expensive scotch by the case. Now what's up?"

"I've been getting some interesting calls from old contacts for the last few days."

"Military?"

"Not yet, but if there is an alphabet agency I haven't heard from, I'd be surprised." His fellow ex-ranger smiled. "Since you're such a bastard when it comes to working with the government on anything but search and recovery, they are hoping I can smooth the way."

Tek leaned back and hit his head against his chair several times. The government always wanted glimpses into his customers' systems. National security was a favorite catch phrase they loved to throw around. Tek had a strict policy, without a court order, he wouldn't even give confirmation someone was his client.

He had customers on the technology side of the house that were on the gray side of the law, including his MC the Dark Sons. He wouldn't work for anyone who he thought was into drugs or human trafficking, but those were his only hard limits. It didn't make him popular with Uncle Sam, but it was funny how quickly they changed their tune when they needed someone found and rescued on the ass end of the globe.

"What company do they want us to turn on now?" Tek almost didn't care since he knew his answer.

"Not a company this time. They all want to subcontract one of our employees." Kane's face showed the puzzlement he felt.

Vallier only hired the best, but to his knowledge they didn't employ anyone so special a bidding war might start in the government. "Your side of the house or Lisen's?"

"Lisen's. I haven't even heard the name before. Angela Turner."

Tek racked his brain but couldn't place the name. He didn't know all the over five hundred employees who worked for him in one way or another, but he thought he was aware of the best. He pressed the intercom on his phone. "Karen, can you have Lisen come to my office and bring me the employment file for an Angela Turner?"

"She's waiting out here and says she has the file."

"Send her in." Tek raised an eyebrow at Kane.

He shrugged and smiled. "I gave her a small heads up."

Lisen opened the door and Tek admired once again that his CIO was what one would call the complete package. With dark exotic looks, which could be on any runway, she was also one of the smartest and most brutal businesspeople he knew. He might have even tried dating her, if it wasn't for the fact she preferred her men and sometimes women on their knees and preferably wearing only a ball gag.

She held up a slim file. "Okay, Kane. You trying to punk me?"

He held up his hands. "I like my balls comfortably outside a vise. I wouldn't dare."

She tossed the folder onto Tek's desk with disgust. "Flyboy here pops in, says 'we have a situation' and that I should pull some woman's file and get to your office. Imagine my surprise when the file is for an intern who hasn't even got her login credentials yet. If this is about some booty call you two are planning, I will not be amused." Lisen rested her hip on his desk and gave Kane a glare that would shrink most men's spines.

Tek flipped open the file and found a one-page resume and the forms for the basic background check they ran on all interns. No red flags on the top page. Twenty-six with a PhD in Psychology from Harvard and ScD in Computer Science from MIT. Both earned before she turned twenty. Her employment history was sparse, only containing internships at several of the leading Tech companies in the country. HR stated they had contacted them all and each company had given her glowing recommendations and had indicated they would hire her back.

It made no sense. Those degrees alone would have made her a prime candidate for employment at any major corporation. Tek typed her name into an internet search engine. Hundreds of articles popped up with her name in the headline. Most were over two years old, but the number alone was impressive. why hadn't he heard of her? The most recent headline read: *Millionaire Prodigy Vanishes After Father's Tragic Death*. "Well, that's interesting," Tek mumbled.

"What?" Lisen snapped.

"Someone in HR is either getting a bonus or fired."

He scrolled through the search pages, reading the highlights. Lisen and Kane came around and looked over his shoulder.

"This girl is one of the pioneers of data mining algorithms and she took a 27k job here doing scut work for data security? We sure it's the same person?" Lisen's eyes narrowed as he settled on a link. The woman had a Wikipedia page dedicated to her.

Tek shrugged as he compared the resume to the tiny entry on the screen. "If it's not her, then it's someone using her credentials." He clicked back and hit the images button. The only pictures he found were of a young teenage girl in a cap and gown with her face turned away from the camera. "Do we have a photo of her?"

"She should get her badge today or tomorrow, but I doubt we have anything yet." Kane moved back to the chair he had been sitting in. "So, there is an undercover millionaire genius working as an intern. There has to be more to her story if the government wants her so bad. Both the NSA and CIA hinted they would pay in the six-figure range for just a few weeks of her time."

Lisen pulled out her phone. "I'll make some calls and dig around a bit. See what I can find. Do you want me to pull her aside?"

"I don't want to spook her before we know why she's here. Put key logging software on any computers she has access to and keep our exposure to a minimum until we learn what's going on. It says here she had a company reference from Joshua Witten." Tek closed his eyes for a second thinking. "I know that name."

"Jojo?" Lisen had laughter in her voice. "Oh, if Jojo aka Joshua is her reference then I can definitely get the scoop."

"Is he the one who did the tribute to a generation of Divas at last year's Christmas party?" Kane asked.

"Yup, and he/she is one of the best encryption specialists we have."

Tek considered what his CIO was saying. "So you're saying she's the real thing?"

"No, I'm saying if he asked me to hire a hamster to work in legal I would probably do it just to keep him happy and most of HR knows that. So they probably didn't check too deep into her background. I'll talk to him and see what he says about her."

Tek swore and closed the folder. "Fine, we'll watch for

now. Both of you see what you can find out and get me a picture of her before my 'get to know you' meeting with the interns this afternoon. We'll meet tomorrow and figure out a game plan. If she's some sort of prodigy, I'm not going to have her working on GUI bugs for our credit check program. If she's a fake, I want her gone before she can do any real damage."

This company may have strayed from his original vision, but there was no way he would allow a liar or government spy to infiltrate his company.

Chapter 7

Some people just need a high five… In the face… With a chair.

The headache building behind her temples had one of two causes; the monumental force she was using to keep her mouth shut or the sound of the stupidity Rick was spouting off. Either way, if she didn't get away from him soon, she would probably explode. The slight break she had gotten when someone from HR had shown up to take her picture for badging hadn't been nearly long enough.

He had sat her at her new desk in the open environment workplace and then went on about how important his team was and how they rarely got 'stuck' with interns. She looked around at the five other programmers who made up his team and noticed not a single one had looked up from their terminal the entire time this windbag talked. It was interesting he hadn't introduced any of them or ever given credit in his stories of their brilliant achievements to anyone but himself. Rick asked several insulting ways what her connection to

Joshua was or if the connection was elsewhere. He was currently telling her how he doubted she could keep up, but he would do his best to mentor her. His tone on that subject made her want to throw up a bit.

"Okay, Angie, let's figure out what skills you have so I can best figure out how to use you." He winked. Her brain froze for a moment and then confirmed, yes, he had just said that.

"D-did you know studies show most women dislike being called a n-nickname by someone they don't have a positive emotional connection with? And th-that most men use nicknames to create the appearance of friendship when it d-doesn't exist?"

Rick stared at her blankly, then gave a fake chuckle. "Okay, Angela." He drew out her name like it was a joke. "What programming languages are you familiar with?"

If the moron had bothered to read her resume, he wouldn't need to ask. Time to channel her father. When asked a stupid question, be sure not to give a stupid answer. "Imperative or Declarative?" She gave herself a pat on the back at the confused look on his face. "I mean technically there are languages like Assembly that might be considered both dependent on the usage. But come on, who uses those anymore except for d-direct hardware manipulation? But to answer your question I have p-programmed or analyzed code in over 40 languages but most companies need people who can code in Java, Python, or Ruby. Which I can. Doesn't it feel like after the 10th or so language it is only a matter of syntax not really a new language?"

A laugh, that was immediately covered by a cough, came from somewhere in the room. She tilted her head as if considering. She continued, "But m-my specialty is optimization algorithms. Hey, you might know the answer to something I've been dying to learn. Do your current data mining programs use Round Robin or FCFS scheduling when running through data?"

Rick stood and left like his pants were on fire. "Sounds like you will be fine. I'm sure Chaz can answer any questions you have on specific problems. Read over your new hire packet, login to all your accounts to make sure they work and don't forget you have orientation later at the conference room I showed you earlier."

Angela tried not to smirk, but it was hard. She looked around the room for a second, took a deep breath, and asked, "Uhm so which one of you is Chaz?"

A thin man in his late thirties waved from a few desks down, his smile almost busting off his face. "Name is Charles. That was epic. Though not the smartest move since our lord and master likes to hold grudges."

She winced but had already figured that. "G-Good to know."

"Oh and as you probably know we use both Round Robin and First Come First Serve dependent on the workload and performance required."

Angela gave a thumbs-up to Charles. She couldn't bring herself to say anything since that info was something only a newbie wouldn't know. The question was to test Rick. His non-answer stated loud and clear he was not the expert he claimed.

She took a deep breath. Getting through the mind-numbing account set up would be easy. One hour and she would finally get to meet the mysterious man behind the company. Joseph Vallier, the only man who might be harder to get a picture of than herself. She had barely resisted the urge to hack the DMV to get an image. Some mysteries were worth the wait.

Chapter 8

The geek is strong with this one.

Tek toggled off the video feed, shaking his head. Every security camera could record sound, though usually the microphones were turned off. Listening in on his employees felt wrong, but the technology came in handy at times like this. The angle of the camera was from the ceiling and only showed the tops of their heads. So, he hadn't gotten a better look at this mystery woman.

"That guy Rick is an ass." Kane stated the obvious.

"Yeah, but he gets shit done." Tek rubbed his neck and pulled up the photo HR had sent of Angela Turner.

"How, by pissing off his staff so bad they work faster to make him go away?" Kane looked at the picture and whistled. "And I thought my badging photo was bad."

Tek couldn't argue with either of his comments. In the picture Angela looked sort of like a bad caricature of Morticia Addams with squinty eyes. Her black hair was covering half her face, and she looked washed out. There was something about the shape of her face which nagged at him. She looked almost familiar somehow.

"The geek talk smack down was kind of hot."

"And means if she isn't Angela, then she is someone who knows what she is talking about. If it is her, we need a plan to keep her." Tek had spent most of the morning avoiding thinking about the potential issue with security and researching Angela.

Her published papers were nothing like the usual dry academic ego stroking. Her theories on using psychology of the designers to predict the strengths and weakness of design within systems were groundbreaking. He knew he was only scratching the surface of her ideas.

Kane raised an eyebrow. "What makes her so special?"

"On paper she is just another talented, well-educated programmer. But when you dig deeper, there is a pattern that is impossible to discount. Look at this."

Kane came around the desk to look at his monitors. "I see lines and numbers."

"It's cute when you try to play dumb. These are the stock prices for the companies she worked as an intern for. Several months after she left each, they had a massive jump that correlates with the release of an upgrade to the software product she worked on." Tek gave Kane a moment to glance over the numbers before switching screens. "These are the patents she holds and these are the government contracts she was listed on as a subject matter expert. If I was looking at the number of patents alone, I would assume she was in her late fifties. But she is only twenty-six. Think of what she could do."

A notification popped up from the software he had monitoring Angela's computer. Tek clicked and a window on his screen opened that mirrored her monitor.

"Going to watch her set up her accounts?" Kane raised an eyebrow.

They watched as her e-mail program popped up.

To: TechnicalSupport@VallierTechnologies.com

Subject: Possible security breach

To whom it may concern,

While installing the programs directed in the new hire packet, I noticed several processes running on my desktop that are outside what I would expect from a fresh install. After doing a trace-back, it would appear that there is key logging and monitoring software installed on my computer. If this is expected, please let me know. I have attached the trace-backs and process names for your confirmation.

Regards,

Angela Turner

Intern Vallier Technologies

Kane burst out laughing and hit Tek on the shoulder. "Guess the stealthy approach won't work."

Tek couldn't help but chuckle. This woman was sharp and a puzzle he wanted to figure out. "Guess not." His phone beeped an alarm. "I'll have to try the more direct approach. Time to welcome the new hires." He stood smiling. "I'll just have to talk to her myself and see what I can find out."

Chapter 9

Welcome to the shit show. We're happy to have you.

One hour left on her first day. Crappy boss... check. Mind numbing account setup complete... check. All that was left was to listen to the 'welcome to our company' speech and then she could head home with Joshua and decide if there would be a day two. The department she was in didn't do any of the interesting work she wanted to be part of. Instead focused on the corporate clients' internal security software.

There were around twenty other people milling around the modern conference room, all younger than her and in much better moods. The one highlight of today would be meeting Joseph Vallier, the man behind the company. Doing her best to fade into the background, Angela took a seat in the corner and didn't make eye contact with any of her fellow new hires. Everyone found a seat, and the lights dimmed for a video about what it meant to be part of Vallier Technologies.

Angela tuned out the movie. She had done her research on the company; it was why she was here. The photos on the website had only included group shots, none of which contained the executives. What type of man would the CEO be? She had gotten a degree in psychology for the sole purpose of better understanding people and why they did things. A CEO who didn't want the publicity was a riddle.

If he was anything like his programs, he would be elegant. Angela snorted at the notion. Joseph was probably a pale, skinny, middle-aged geek. The lights came up, and she forgot to breathe.

A sharp pain shot through her chest. The sexy, gray-eyed man from last night stood at the front of the room. His well chiseled physique, beautifully contained within a black, button-down shirt and gray slacks which had to be custom tailored to display his legs so well. She would have bolted from the room if every muscle in her body hadn't locked up in shock.

"I'm Joseph Vallier." He gave a smile that caused her stomach to flutter. "Working at this company should be about more than the paycheck. Making the world a safer place is our goal, and each of you should want to be a part of that. I like to meet every employee and find out why they chose to work here rather than somewhere else. Let's go around the room, I want each of you to introduce yourself and tell me what you think you can contribute." His voice was unmistakable. Deep and rich, it had filled her dreams last night.

How was this possible? Of all the men in the world, how was he her new boss? Okay, her many times removed boss, but still. Angela's ears buzzed as the people around the room introduced themselves, their words bouncing off her brain like raindrops. Oh God, would he recognize her?

She was wearing a wig and had all her clothes on, so maybe not. Should she try to disguise her voice? She could fake a seizure… pretend to be mute… The last idea had merit. Maybe spontaneous laryngitis was a thing. This couldn't be happening to her!

"Ms. Turner?" His voice snapped her out of her panic.

She popped up out of her seat and said the first thing that came to her mind, "I'm Angela Turner. I wanted to work here because I would like to optimize your search algorithms for subject acquisition to use behavioral models in selecting prioritization of data processing." She dropped back into her seat, her whole-body heating with embarrassment. Praying the floor would swallow her.

Joseph, or should she think of him as Tek, smiled. "That is an interesting idea." His head cocked, and he studied her. "Do you have experience with that kind of work?"

Her legs squeezed together as his crisp business tone reminded her too vividly of last night. "Yes, Sir."

"You seem familiar. Have we met?" She bit her lip, praying he wouldn't place her, but his eyes widened for a moment and she knew that wish would be unfulfilled.

She nodded. Oh God, she was going to die. Spontaneous combustion or a stroke anything to make this end. Running was a thought, but though she was in shape, his legs were longer. At the moment, she barely remembered where the door was. Finding a path out of the building was unlikely without being caught.

His small, knowing smile was unfairly sexy. "I'd love to hear your ideas on optimization. Please stay after the meeting and we can discuss them."

She really doubted he had any intention of discussing business. While parts of her body were totally on board with listening to anything he had to say, her brain was sure the statistics on mixing her carnal goals with her work ones were dismal. Tek continued on with a canned speech which was probably moving and important, but she didn't hear a word of it.

Would he try to reenact last night, only replace secretary with intern? The idea was tempting. Maybe he would fire her because of her side job? That would make the decision on whether or not to stay much easier. Tek's voice raised slightly, and she focused back on the front of the room. "It was wonderful meeting you all. Welcome to Vallier Technologies. I look forward to all your great work."

Everyone clapped and stood to leave. The air in the room seemed to thin and Angela had a hard time breathing. She couldn't stay and face him. Whatever he wanted to say would have to wait till later. Or never. Never worked for her.

She waited till Tek turned his head to answer the question of one of the other new hires and snuck through the crowd out into the hall. Her heart pounded against her chest as she picked up her pace. This whole place was too open-concept to hide. Wait, there to the right. A door that wasn't an office. She grabbed the handle and ducked into the room.

Shelves of paper and office supplies lined the small closet that, thank goodness, had a light. She paced the three steps she could and held back the scream that wanted to crawl out of her throat. Why had she run? Okay she knew why but this was not part of the new confident and under control her. So what if her new boss had seen her dancing on stage and made her orgasm at his command? She wasn't ashamed, was she? Pulling out her phone, she texted Joshua.

Me: *Help! I'm hiding in the 3rd floor supply closet.*

A minute passed before her phone dinged a response.

Joshua: *I didn't know you were in the closet. Does this mean you are coming out?*

Me: *Ha Ha. No, I'm never coming out of the closet.*

Joshua: *Oh sweetie. I love you no matter what your orientation.*

Before she could figure out a way to strangle her friend through the phone, the door to the room opened. She relaxed, assuming her friend had come to save her from herself. Her breath caught in her lungs as she looked up.

No such luck.

Chapter 10

You can't make good decisions without experience, and you can't have experience without bad decisions.

Tek closed the supply room door and leaned back against it, studying the sight in front of him. It was hard to believe this woman was the same temptress he had met last night. Instead of confident and sexy, she stood in the back of the closet looking like a cornered rabbit. The new look was interesting. The black wig she wore was high quality and the suit obviously designer, but the shocked look in her teal-blue eyes was almost comic. Was she just hiding from him because of embarrassment, or was it something more?

Tek had been frustrated when he noticed Angela had snuck out of the room without talking to him, but a helpful employee had told him he saw the new girl duck in the supply closet. He had started the orientation meeting with several questions for this puzzle of a woman, and now he had so many more. He started with the simplest.

"Why did you run away from me?"

He could almost see the gears turning behind her expressive eyes. She took a deep breath and seemed to steady. "I d-did not run, Mr. Vallier. I attempted to a-avoid an unnecessary awkward conversation."

He couldn't help but chuckle at her haughty tone of voice. He stepped forward and enjoyed the way her breath shuddered, and her nipples visibly tightened under her blouse. "So formal, Ms. Turner. But I hadn't planned to have an awkward conversation with you in the very public conference room."

"Oh." She looked around; eyes gone wide. "We're not in p-public. Does that mean you're going to fire me here? I've never been f-fired before. Is it usually done in p-private?"

She was adorable and sexy in a mix that was irresistible to him. Even her stutter was a perfect tell which let him know she was as affected as he was. He crossed his arms, fighting the urge to close the distance between them. "Why would I be firing you?"

A beautiful pink shade filled her cheeks. "Because of last night?"

Tek's lips twitched in an amused smile. "I quite enjoyed last night."

She swayed towards him for a second, her lips parted as if remembering what had happened between them. It took all of his willpower to keep his distance.

She blinked as if coming back to herself. "I m-mean because I'm a s-stripper."

"And I go to strip clubs. It would be hypocritical of me to fire you for that."

"Well, the world isn't really known for its lack of hypocrisy and statistically it is the woman who is held to higher standards. You c-can't really blame me for thinking that might be the case here."

It was adorable the way she was stumbling over her

thoughts. Cute wasn't a quality that Tek would have thought of as desirable, but everything about her worked for him. She licked her lips, and he wanted to know what she tasted like.

Her hair had fallen down in front of her eyes and he wanted to brush it back so he could see her face clearly.

"I don't hold people to double standards."

"That's good." She looked up and bit her lip. "Why did you follow me?"

"I found out today I had an overly qualified intern working for me. Did some research and found out she is highly desired by all sorts of people." Tek enjoyed the blush his suggestive words caused. "I had to meet her and see if there was anything I could do to seduce her into taking a more hands-on position with the company."

"I-I well uhm. Thank you. But I d-don't like the stress of commitment. I like to be free to do who I want. I mean what I want." She slapped her hand over her mouth as if she just realized how her words could be taken.

Tek laughed and enjoyed the freeing sensation. It had been a long time since someone made him truly smile at something so simple as a slip of the tongue.

"Good to know. What made you choose to work for my company?"

"I told you at the meeting."

He quirked an eyebrow. "Optimization of search algorithms?"

Her face seemed to come alive, all hints of shyness gone. "Not just any algorithms, the ones used to prioritize data source selection when searching for criminals or missing people. Have you heard of the behavioral modeling research being done for AI?" She started pacing in the small room. "Of course, you have. Well, if you were to combine that along with the current criminal profiling logic you could predict probabilities of movement, purchasing behavior, and use the data to prioritize what databases to search decreasing the time it would take to find anything there is to find on your subject." Her eyes were sparkling with excitement, her stutter missing when talking with passion.

"You make it sound easy," Tek teased.

"No, not easy." She stopped her pacing and stood only inches from him, looking up with a serious expression. "It would take several months of work and resources, but the result would possibly save lives. That's what you do here, why I want to help."

Her words sparked something inside him that had been pushed aside for years. The reason he had created the company in the first place. Profit had replaced passion, and he wanted that sense of purpose back.

He wanted to fan her brilliance and be part of her success. How could one person challenge him mentally, reignite his passion to make a difference and tempt his body? Tek stroked a finger down her cheek. He rolled the hair of her wig between his fingers, enjoying her tiny gasp. "Why the wig?"

"I was trying to be professional." Her deep breath had her chest brushing his. She looked up and her breath mingled with his own. "I wanted to impress my new boss."

He cupped her cheek, knowing that what he was doing was not smart. Her passion and physical pull on him was almost too much. He needed the answer to at least one more question. "Did you know who I was last night?"

"No."

Her answer was an exhale of breath and he believed her. "I want to hear all your ideas, really I do, but first I have to know how you taste."

He leaned down and kissed her with the pent-up passion still simmering from last night. The flavor of something sweet mixed with mint was like a drug, pulling him in as her tentative tongue met his in an almost hesitant sweep.

Her hands clutched his shirt and the tiny moans she gave were music to his ears. He ran his hand down her neck, enjoying the way she leaned into his touch like a cat. He swept his hand down her body until her pebbled nipples pressed against his fingers under the silky material of her blouse.

His cock jumped at her throaty moan as he swept his thumb over the tight peaks, alternating as he came up from the kiss so he could see the beauty of her body.

She arched as he pinched her nipples, her body trembling under his touch. His leg was pressed between hers and she had started grinding against it in a pulsing rhythm.

Tek smiled as he continued to tease her nipples. He undid her pants and slipped a hand inside, loving how her wetness covered his fingers. "Last night watching you come without being able to touch you was an exercise in control. I wonder, do you have enough control to not scream as I make you come?"

"Uhm." Angela bit her lip. "I'm not sure this is a good idea."

Her body kept moving against his hand regardless of her words. Tek stilled and nipped her ear.

"You want me to stop, kitten?"

"No!" she gasped and rotated her hips.

Tek found her clit with the tips of his fingers and ran slow circles around it. "Are you scared that there is only a door between us and the rest of the company?"

"No, it's not that."

Tek leaned in, whispering into her ear. "Is this one of your fantasies? The intern being seduced by her boss. Being so swept up in the moment they both forget where they are or what might happen if they are caught." He circled his fingers faster. "I know I ache to be inside you. I want to spend hours learning your body and your dirty, brilliant mind."

Her nails dug into his chest at his words. After hearing

what he had about her roleplaying on stage at Darklights and everything he had learned since, he wondered if she might be an even better match for him than he had thought. He wanted to start here but take his time with her back at his place, exploring all the possibilities.

"That feels so good... Mr. Vallier... Please, I want this, but I don't... I can't... think." Her body was tightening, her words tumbling in sexy, incoherent strings.

He added pressure, brushing her clit instead of just circling it. "Tek. When you come, I want to hear you call my name." Her breathing became gasps. The sounds had him almost ready to come himself. "Tell me how you want me to fuck you, kitten. Give me the dirty words and I'll make every fantasy come true."

Her head fell back as he thrust two fingers into her tight channel. She would be like a vice around his cock, pulling him to orgasm like a teenager in moments. He stroked her clit with his thumb and he felt her walls start to tremble.

Angela's eyes met his, her pupils wide. "I want to experience it all. From the captured harem slave to the naughty schoolgirl. I want the gentle lover and the rough biker who fucks me so hard I ache days later." Her pants began matching his motions. He knew she would come soon. Later he would make her give him all the details of what she wanted. For now, he wanted to see her break apart in his arms. "I just... don't want my first time to be in a supply closet. Oh God... Tek!"

Her body convulsed around his fingers as she muffled her cries into his chest a little too late. The beautiful sight of her shaking in his arms made him slow to process the words she had said.

Her first time?

Chapter 11

When your thought starts with 'Fuck it', what follows is either a really good or bad decision.

The world splintered into shining sparkles with her orgasm. Angela finally understand why people wanted a sexual partner. Orgasms triggered by others were so much more powerful than the ones she had given herself since she discovered them at twenty-one.

She prayed no one had heard her cries but couldn't dredge up too much concern. Even his hand slipping out of her sent extra sparks through her body. If this was what he could do to her in a tiny room with nothing but his hand, she looked forward to finding out what else he was skilled at.

"Kitten?" Tek's voice held a hesitancy causing her to look up into his concerned face. "You mean you don't want our first time to be in a supply closet?"

Was he purposely twisting her words because he didn't believe her or because he didn't want it to be so? She shook her head. Dropping the fact she was a virgin on him indirectly hadn't been a conscious choice. With the speed they connected, she supposed it might be a shock. She'd hoped it wouldn't be an issue, but the growing expression of horror on his face as she remained silent made that unlikely.

He took two quick steps backward, and she felt heat rushing to her cheeks. Awkward conversations were something she should be used to. The joy and good feelings bled out of her body as she straightened and buttoned her clothes. Nerves as usual had words bubbling out of her.

"While it is possible, you are a virgin as well, my request for a change in venue referred solely to my own p-preferences." God, she hated her stutter. "I've been told your first sexual experience should be sp-special. I guess technically, since the majority of the population hasn't experienced sex in a supply closet at work, this might qualify. I would prefer to have a bed or a more relaxing location. I apologize if that disappoints you and am willing—"

A knock at the door interrupted her rambling.

"Honey. Unlock the door." Joshua's concerned voice was slightly muffled.

Angela had completely forgotten she texted her friend to come get her. From the stunned look on Tek's face, it might be for the best. Things were awkward enough and her talking was making things worse. She needed time to process and come up with the best solution that didn't end up with her fired and hopefully led to Tek showing her the other sexual wonders she had been missing out on.

"One minute, Joshua." Angela lowered her voice. "He is my ride. I called him before you joined me in here."

"Yeah." Tek ran his hands through his hair. "I need to… we can talk later."

Her stomach dropped as the man she was so attracted to spun and left the closet like he was being chased by rabid dogs.

Would they ever talk, or was it just polite nonsense? It would be understandable if he avoided her. She had made things awkward. Not that she regretted speaking up. No matter how sexy and talented Tek was, she would regret if they rushed and ruined a memory she would retain for life.

"You have some explaining to do, sweetheart." Joshua leaned against the doorway, a mischievous grin on his face that made her smile.

"Can it wait till we are in the car?"

He raised an eyebrow. "Only if we are leaving right this second."

"That works for me."

She felt the eyes of the people working near the supply closet boring into her skin. What had they heard? Was she about to become the center of gossip? Fear and frustration swirled in her stomach, and she was unprepared to think about what her moment of passion might have cost her. To her relief Joshua was good to his word, staying silent until they were pulling out of the parking lot.

"Spill."

The single word released the floodgates on her mouth and emotions. She explained about the private dance and the attraction, then the crappy first day ending in seeing her fantasy man up at the front of the employee orientation.

"So let me get this straight. You unknowingly danced naked for your hot new boss, then the next day ended up alone in a supply closet with him?"

Angela blushed. "Yeah."

"And if I hadn't interrupted?"

"You didn't interrupt anything exactly."

"Uh-huh. Honey, I know the look of a man who has been cock-blocked. And that gorgeous piece of candy had sexual frustration written all over his face."

Angela crossed her arms. "I wasn't going to lose my virginity in a supply closet."

Joshua's laughter filled the car. "Did you tell him that?"

"Yes."

"Oh girl, you are too much. How did he take it?"

"I think not so well. He was a little shocked." Probably more than a little. Things had moved so fast and she wasn't sure. Maybe she could do something nice for him. Hallmark didn't make 'Sorry I left you with blue-balls' cards but it couldn't be his first time being left wanting.

Her friend patted her knee, breaking off the odd thoughts. "I know I tease you about getting out there, but Joseph Vallier is heartbreak wrapped up in a gorgeous package. How much do you know about him?"

"Not much." Though she would be fixing that the moment she got home.

"I have worked at Vallier for years and in all that time I've never heard of him dating. Rumor is he is married to the mission. He built the company so no one ever has to go through what he did."

"What happened?" She remembered reading something about a family tragedy and now regretted not looking deeper. Sometimes her logic overrode her heart when she was in the middle of research.

"Someone kidnapped his sister from a playground. They never found her or who took her. All the money in the world and there was nothing his parents could do."

Angela's chest tightened as sorrow wrapped around her. That was the ultimate nightmare. Not knowing would be worse than any grief. "That's horrible, but what does it have to do with now?"

"They say his life is the company and his motorcycle club. Many women have tried, but his heart doesn't have room for anything else."

She could understand that. Grief at losing her father had overwhelmed almost two years of her life. Not knowing would be so much worse. Maybe she could help him find closure. She had worked on a project three years ago which revolutionized photo aging using genetic markers. If she combined that with a search of obituaries, coroner reports, and driver's licenses, she might be able to find out his sister's fate.

Joshua groaned. "That does not look like the expression of someone taking good advice. "

Angela shrugged. "I understand what you're saying."

"But you are going to do you." Joshua sighed. "Well, know this, honey, no matter what happens I'm here for you."

If they hadn't been driving, Angela would have given her friend the hug the statement deserved. She might even take his advice, but something inside her told her what was going on between her and Tek was far from over.

Chapter 12

If gossip was chocolate, we'd all be overweight.

itting at the bar, the whisky burned Tek's throat. He couldn't corral his thoughts into any sense of order. The sounds of Dark Sons relaxing filled the room as it did around dinner most nights. The Clubhouse was a large building on an isolated property outside of Denver which functioned as a home, party central, and a meeting place for all the Brothers. He had come here trying to escape the problems at work and the complete mess he had made of interrogating Angela. Fuck, he could barely keep his dick from taking over and hunting her down. How could a woman that sexy be a virgin?

The things he wanted to do to her were not fit for an innocent. She was a stripper, a genius, and a millionaire. Was she really inexperienced or was it another part of her roleplay? Complicated wasn't supposed to be his thing.

"Heya, Tek. What has you looking so serious?" A tiny

shoulder bumped into his side and he looked over to see Pixie sliding into the barstool to his right.

Pixie was a tiny, blonde, pregnant bundle of joy. You would never guess she had seen more horrors in her life than most combat hardened military men. His Brother Sharp had saved her and claimed her as his Old Lady, which was more sacred than marriage among bikers. The two lovebirds were soon to be parents if the size of Pixie's belly was any indication. She had quickly worked her way into all the Brothers' hearts by making sure every weeknight there was a fantastic home cooked meal waiting for anyone who wanted to join.

Tek felt a connection to her that had never been sexual but was strong. He smiled at her. "Work crap. How is the munchkin treating you?"

"He is fond of kicking at all hours. Six more weeks to go." She rubbed her belly.

"Sharp treating you right?"

"You know he is. No distracting me. That is the look of someone worrying about more than quarterly statements. I'll back off if you want, but I worry about you."

The concerned expression on her face surprised him. His Brothers looked out for him but they didn't worry. The last woman who had cared enough to poke at him was his mother before his sister disappeared, tearing the family apart.

"Thanks for caring, Pixie, but it's nothing I can't handle."

"You hitting on my woman?" Sharp walked up and wrapped an arm around his woman, placing a kiss on top of her head. He gave Tek a chin lift in greeting.

Tek smiled, winking at Pixie. "Of course I am. Need to make sure she makes my favorite cookies."

She rolled her eyes. "I was just trying to figure out what had your grumpy Brother sulking. All work and no play makes Tek a miserable man."

Was that how people saw him? It was true he hadn't been

around much the last few months except for official club business. Even now he knew he should be back at work figuring out what was going on with the possible security breaches or digging deeper into Angela. Instead, he was fighting off fantasies of what he wanted to do to her. Her revelation and lack of experience was both a temptation and a hindrance. A primal part of him wanted nothing more than to claim that innocence for himself. Wanted to be her one and only.

Fuck, was he really thinking he might want her for more than a few fun nights?

"I hear he has his eye on one of the Darklights' girls." Sharp smirked.

Tek flipped his friend off. "We a bunch of gossiping grannies now?"

"Oh, who is it?" Pixie giggled, and the sound was too innocent. Tek and all the Brothers knew that under her pixie-like appearance was a wild woman. Maybe his Angela would be the same.

His Angela? He needed to stop thinking about her in that way. Tek gave Sharp a harsh look that didn't even dim the man's smile.

"Hawk said it's one of the new girls. Tammy or Amy."

"Cami," Tek growled.

Pixie clapped. "So you do like her?"

He realized his mistake too late as Sharp chuckled. Coming here had been such a mistake. Instead of getting her off his mind, he was talking about her. If gossip spread like fire between the Brothers, it would go nuclear once their Old Ladies got a hold of it.

"I'm not in high-school, short-stuff. Don't you have dinner to be finishing up?"

"Oh, he's defensive, must be something special."

His phone rang and with an annoyed glare at Pixie, he answered without looking at who was calling. "Yeah?"

Pixie held her hands up in surrender, sliding out of her chair. The two troublemakers backed away with grins. He knew it meant he had plenty more shit coming his way later.

"You sound pleasant. How you make the big bucks with that attitude is beyond me." Lisen's chiding tone did nothing to settle his nerves.

"Yeah, well, unless you want me to stop paying you the big bucks, tell me why you're calling."

"Someone needs to get laid, stat."

"Lisen," Tek growled, letting all his frustration out in one word.

"If this wasn't important, I'd tell you to go fuck yourself, but it is." The sound of her taking a deep breath had his stomach dropping. "It's confirmed. Someone hacked Tribeca conglomerates and leaked internal proposal numbers to their competitors. We need you in the office now."

Chapter 13

Character is like pregnancy; it cannot be hidden forever. -African Proverb

Going to work the next day was an exercise in determination. She had stayed up most of the night researching Tek's missing sister and creating the different age mock-ups from age four to twenty-one. Her data mining programs were set to match photos on all the accessible legal databases. She estimated the search would take three days. If nothing came back, she would try less legal ways of looking.

The upside of being so tired was she didn't care about first impressions anymore. Her job was doomed, so who cared what her co-workers thought. She still wore a professional suit, but her purple hair was swept up into a simple ponytail. Joshua had texted to say he was called in early so she had to drive in by herself.

The atmosphere in the office was completely different from her first day. Instead of calm and friendly, there was tension everywhere. When she made it to her desk, there was a muffin and a sticky note was on her monitor which said 'Don't forget: You Rock!'. She laughed and pulled it off. The note was so Joshua.

The work area was practically deserted, only one person was at their desk.

"Hey Charles, where is everyone?"

He laughed, then raised his eyebrows as he took her in. "Nice hair."

"Thanks."

"Looks better on you than the black." He looked up at the clock on the wall. "It's eight o'clock. Most of the programmers flex and work later in the day. Rick is schmoozing the management types as he does every day. You going to be an early bird like me?"

"I don't think flextime is something interns are allowed to do. So should I email Rick for work?"

"Nah. He already passed off all his actual work to me. If you think you're up to it, I have some fascinating GUI bugs you can dig into." He wiggled his eyebrows as if he was offering her something interesting rather than the nightmare it probably was.

Playing along, she clasped her hands over her heart. "Oh, tell me more!"

"Oh you are going to love this the beta team says that the GUI is and I'm quoting here," Charles paused dramatically, "buggy and slow."

Angela chuckled. "Of course it is."

Five hours later, she was ready to strangle whoever had created the nightmare that was the Log-in GUI. They hadn't used any of the built in JAVA modules, and instead coded their own Frankenstein version of each button. Trace-backs had her rolling her eyes in disbelief. Rather than make things more secure, they had created massive holes in the encryption and bypassed it completely in others.

GUIs were supposed to be an interface with the underlying code, but whoever had made this crap had embedded functions that shouldn't be available to anyone who didn't have the correct encryption keys. If this went live, any data it protected was as good as public knowledge. Hell, she had run some of the code and found herself in databases she probably shouldn't be able to access.

"Team meeting!" Rick's voice cut through her thoughts like a knife.

As Angela followed behind the rest of the team, her stomach growled and reminded her she probably should have stopped for lunch. Rick didn't bother to wait for everyone to sit down before he started in on them.

"Our productivity numbers are down this month. I expect each and every one of you to be putting in extra time to make sure we reach our goals." The collective groan from the team had him scowling. "I don't want to hear it. We have an extra body this month, so I expect us to exceed projections for lines of code."

"You expect an intern who hasn't even been on the system a day to help us catch up in the next week?"

Angela hadn't met the person who spoke yet, so she let her pride settle and kept her mouth shut. She didn't know what their goals were or how far behind they were. If the code she had been looking at all morning was any indication in her mind, it would be faster to start over than fix some of that crap.

Rick's gaze bored into her as if he had heard her thoughts. "How many lines of code have you done this morning, Angie?"

She ground her teeth at the unwanted nickname. This guy was an idiot if his only metric was lined off code produced. It often took hours of debugging and research to produce a few lines to fix existing code. If she was starting something new, it would be different.

"None, I've been trying to make sense of the GUI interface before I try to fix it."

"Who told you to work on the GUI? That is my section of the code."

Well, that definitely explained the nightmare of spaghetti code she had been peeling through.

"I did." Charles spoke up. "You said to handle the trouble tickets. One came in and she knows Java, so I thought it would be a good place for her to start."

Angela snorted.

Rick whirled on Charles. "I've made it clear any work on the GUI was mine. It is my custom code that will make this thing a success. I won't have some intern screwing with it."

Charles put his hands up in surrender. "Sorry. Figured anything she would do would go through inspection so no harm."

Angela took a deep breath, knowing she was probably stepping into something deep but knowing it had to be said. "Rick, I spent the morning studying the code. It is full of inefficiencies, holes, and just plain bad practices."

"Shut up!" He barked at her and she flinched backward. "I don't expect some purple haired wanna-be software intern to understand the complexities of what I created. You may want to wait till you've worked in one place for more than six months and not gotten fired for incompetence before saying you know better than the experts."

The whiplash of anger made no sense. She wanted to scream at him, but all the words froze in her throat. She had never been fired, and she sure as hell had never been accused of incompetence. From the smug, condescending looks on everyone's faces, she figured they believed the lies this guy was spouting.

"I-I h-have n-ne-never-" Damn her stutter.

"Go home, Angie." Rick practically sneered her name. "Come back tomorrow with a better attitude or it won't take me six months to fire you no matter who you are friends with."

His words were like a punch to the gut. Talking was pointless and hitting him with her chair would probably get her arrested, Angela stood grabbed her purse from her desk and with all the dignity she could muster walked towards the elevators.

It was tempting to quit, let the crap code go into production, but she knew it wouldn't be Rick paying for the lapse. If they didn't fix the code, whoever used the program would suffer for his ego.

She texted Joshua.

Me: *Hey need to talk, about to have a meltdown.*

JoJo: *Sorry sweetie stuck in meetings. Big emergency. May not be home tonight. Promise to let you vent for hours about your dick boss when this is over.*

Crap. She really needed to tell someone.

Me: *NP*

JoJo: ***HUGS***

She stepped onto the elevator and had what she knew was a bad idea. She hit the up arrow before she could change her mind.

As she stepped out onto the executive floor, she twisted her hands with nerves. Calm. Cool. Professional. This was a matter that could affect the whole company. Sure she was jumping several levels of escalation but she knew Tek, he would listen. Maybe.

She reached the secretary in front of his closed office doors.

"How may I help you?" The polite and professional blonde smiled at her.

"I n-need to speak to Mr. Vallier."

"I'm sorry he canceled all meetings for today. Were you not contacted?" She gave a sad smile, as if she really was sorry.

"I didn't h-have an appointment."

"Well, I can take a message and contact you if he wants to meet."

Angela's shoulders slumped. This day was not working out for her. "P-Please tell him Angela Turner would like to s-speak with him."

The secretary scribbled her information on a memo pad. She looked at Angela squarely. "Have a nice day."

Angela knew this was as far as she could push it with the secretary. There was no way she was going to speak with Tek today.

Riding down the elevator, Angela rested her head against the cool metal wall. It didn't feel right to leave, but what else could she do?

Chapter 14

An enemy can't betray you, only those you trust.

"I'm telling you, it's too convenient. A world class hacker starts working for us right after we start to have security breaches?" Lisen's words did nothing to help Tek's impending headache.

"I know nothing about hacking, but if she was involved, wouldn't the problems have started after she started not before?" Kane was sprawled on the couch in Tek's office, having decided he needed to stay in the loop.

Lisen was pacing the floor like a caged tiger, making Tek annoyed while he dug through the evidence while his cyber security team sent him updates on what they were finding.

"Maybe she found something she couldn't get from the outside and decided working from our own network was easier."

Tek thought Lisen was taking the whole thing very personally and grabbing at straws. They all were exhausted after pulling an all-nighter. Crappy food and no sleep didn't have any of them in a good mood.

Kane shook his head. "I'm supposed to be the paranoid one. Right now you are making me sound down right reasonable. We don't know she is a hacker. All we know is she is a very talented, young, and beautiful programmer."

Lisen snorted. "Yes, of course. The NSA wants to pay six figures for a few weeks of her time because she is pretty."

Tek growled, cutting Kane's comeback off. "Stop it both of you. Lisen, we will investigate Angela, though I think her an unlikely suspect. Kane, stop baiting Lisen." He read through the latest report, grinding his teeth at the lack of information they held.

"I say we interview her." Lisen leaned down, placing her hands on his desk. "If it's not her, then maybe, if she is so talented, she will understand how the hack was done."

The idea had merit, though Tek didn't want to talk to her while he was still uncertain about his feelings. He needed to focus on what was best for the company. The only thing his security team had found so far was that the encryption hadn't been broken but somehow bypassed. It was not in the best interest of the company to avoid uncomfortable situations, so he nodded.

Kane stood as Lisen practically sprinted for the door. "I'm coming with you."

"Think I can't handle her on my own?" Lisen glared at Kane.

"No. Trying to save the company a lawsuit if you decide to break out the restraints and your flogger to get her to talk."

The image of Angela bound and being flogged had his dick jumping to attention. The things he would do to her tied down and at his mercy were almost endless. He shook his head. This was not the time to lose himself in his fantasies. He would use the time they were gone to try to recreate the hack. He was barely into connecting to the network from an outside workstation when Lisen stormed back through his door.

"She's gone." At Lisen's proclamation, he looked at the time. Barely three o'clock.

"What do you mean she's gone?"

Kane strolled in after the angry woman, an unhappy look on his face. "Rick sent her home early."

The smug smile on Lisen's face wasn't attractive. "She is disruptive, doesn't respect authority, and apparently can't code on the level we require here. He asked for permission to fire her."

Tek had heard enough. He pinched his nose, trying to stay calm. "Lisen. what the fuck crawled up your ass about this girl?"

"Well, that is what he said." Her response was defensive, there had to be more behind her attitude.

"You didn't even know who she was yesterday, but today you act as if she is Satan personified. You have flip-flopped between her being a world class hacker to incompetent. We're dealing with a problem that could cost the company millions and ruin our reputation. If we don't figure out what happened soon, there won't be a digital division of Vallier Technologies left. So please just spit it out."

Tek stared at his longtime friend and waited her out. When she finally spoke, each word was clipped and spoken through gritted teeth. "I can't stand women who try to sleep their way to the top."

Tek leaned back in his chair, stunned. Kane's response was faster. "What the fuck?"

Lisen threw her hands up in the air, finally losing some of her anger. "It's not so big of a company. Everyone on the third floor is talking about how she lured you into a supply closet on her first day and you left it pissed and obviously turned on."

Tek groaned, running his hands over his face in frustration. Okay, following her into the supply closet had been stupid. His little head wasn't the best decision maker. He did not have time for this bullshit.

"I'm going to say this once. She did not lure me anywhere. I followed her after she ran away from me. If she was sleeping her way to the top, I wouldn't have left the room still visibly turned on." Kane laughed and Lisen actually looked embarrassed. "Back to the point. If she was a fake who can't code, the government wouldn't even know who she was. Rick is a dick who doesn't like people who don't fall for his charms."

Kane cleared his throat. "We should still eliminate her as a suspect. If she is in on this, then Joshua might be too."

"No way. I would bet my life on his loyalty." Lisen shook her head.

Kane sat back down on the couch. "She could have fooled him, used his knowledge to start the hack, then used him to get the job here."

"Now you think she did it?" Tek's head was spinning from all the quick turns in logic.

"Not really. But someone needs to play devil's advocate and since Lisen has backed down, that is now my job."

Kane's words circled in Tek's mind for hours. The two had finally left his office. It was nine o'clock before he finally gave up on trying to recreate the hack. It was time to investigate what Angela had been doing on the system to eliminate her from the suspect pool. He pulled up the results from the traces on her system and studied them. The blood drained from his face. She had been in the very databases that had been compromised. Resigned, he called Joshua up to his office.

Joshua strode in with an energy the man shouldn't have

had since he had been called in last night and probably hadn't slept in over twenty-four hours. "Hey boss man. I don't have any new news for you. We are working every angle but still don't know how they bypassed my encryption. We've shut-down the servers for now, but the customer won't be happy if it stays that way for too long."

"Not why I called you up here."

Joshua sat down in the chair in front of Tek's desk and crossed his legs. "Color me intrigued. Why am I here?"

"How well do you know Angela?"

"Better than most. In fact better than I know you." The man's defensive tone let Tek know he needed to step carefully.

"You understand talking to her about your work could lose you your clearance. It would take us months to get her cleared and we don't do that for interns."

Joshua crossed his arms. "Let me get this straight. You think I might have told her something she isn't cleared for on this super-secret government trial?"

Tek was tired. Dancing around the fact was a waste of time, so he nodded.

Joshua rolled his eyes. "Honey, I know you just met my girl, but you should do your homework. Angela not only has higher government clearance than my paltry secret, I'm pretty sure she has higher clearance than most Generals do." He raised a hand as if cutting Tek off. "But before you get your panties all twisted, no, I've never discussed the details of my work with her."

"I need to talk with her."

"It's Thursday night she won't be home till after midnight."

What did it being Thursday have to do with anything? It wasn't like it was a party night. Tek shook his head as he remembered her other job. More caffeine would be necessary if he was going to get through this investigation.

She would be at Darklights. Thoughts of her dancing on stage again had his cock responding before his brain could stop it.

It sucked he was attracted to the woman who could be about to destroy the company he had spent his life creating.

Chapter 15

Sometimes life is like a lemon. So bright and pretty on the outside but bitter and sour on the inside.

S he should have called in sick. Hell, she probably should have quit. Angela wasn't feeling like Cami anymore. Her dances had been lackluster at best, and there was no way she could do the private tonight. She saw Decaf as she was walking down the hall to the dressing room and admitted defeat.

"Hey Decaf?"

"Yeah, Cami?" The tall, well-built biker gave her a friendly smile.

"Can you tell Clean I'm not doing the private tonight?" She'd never realized how strange these men's names were. It was odd that only when she planned to never see them again was when she considered how they had gotten their nicknames.

"He's not going to be happy. Most of the men out there

came for the chance of getting a private dance with you."
Decaf's scowl made her waver, but she couldn't go through
with it.

"Sorry." She shook her head. "I can't. I'm pretty sure that
was my last dance."

"What's going on? I know stripping isn't the most glam-
orous job in the world, but you're damn good at it." Decaf
gave her a small smile. "And hey, it pays the bills."

She appreciated his words but had to laugh. "It doesn't
pay my bills."

"If you need more cash, Clean would love to have you do
more nights."

"I meant I don't need the money." She shook her head,
knowing she shouldn't be revealing so much.

"Okay. I'll let him know."

"Thanks. I'm going to go change. If he wants to talk to
me, that's where I'll be." Angela turned and headed into the
locker room.

Jasmine was sitting at the mirror touching up her makeup
when Angela walked in the small room.

"How's your daughter?"

"Much better." Jasmine smiled at her. "It was a double ear
infection. One day on antibiotics and you wouldn't even know
she had been sick. Thank you so much for the loan. I'll pay
you back as soon as I can. Clean is going to give me some
extra shifts, so it shouldn't be long."

"About that. I really don't want you to pay me back. Think
of it as paying it forward. You see someone else who needs
help, then you help them."

"Someone did that for you?" The woman didn't seem to
believe her.

She remembered Jojo showing up in all her drag queen
glory to drag her out of her mourning every night for months.
If it hadn't been for her friend, she would still be hiding away

from the world, living off delivered meals, and afraid of talking to anyone. "Yeah, they did. Changed my life. Besides, you probably won't see me again. T-tonight was my last performance."

"You serious?" When Angela nodded, Jasmine sighed. "You always were too classy for this place."

"You saying my place isn't classy?" Clean's mellow midwestern tone had Angela jumping.

"Not what I meant, Boss, and you know it." Jasmine smirked.

Well, that was fast. Angela bit her lip, not wanting to get in an argument with the manager of Darklights. She knew things about the man that she shouldn't. When she had researched the club, she had created files on each of the employees. To most people, he was a ghost that had only come into existence a few years ago. The classified information she had found on a CIA server was horrifying and tragic. It needed to stay buried, and she had made sure of that.

She plastered a smile on, sinking into her role as Cami before turning around. "Hey, Clean."

"Jasmine, can you give us the room?"

"Sure, Boss." Jasmine stood and hugged her. "In case I don't get to say it later, goodbye, good luck, and thank you."

Cami hugged her back, surprised at how sad she felt at saying goodbye. When it was only Clean and her in the room, he gestured for her to sit. She grabbed her robe and wrapped it around herself, not wanting to have a serious conversation in only her bra and panties.

"I got an interesting call from Tek earlier telling me to put him on the list for your private dance."

Those words shouldn't have made her happy, but they did. Maybe she hadn't blown her chance with the disastrous supply closet scene. "Oh?" Brilliant conversationalist, that was her.

"He the reason you're quitting?"

"No." Well, probably indirectly, but it didn't matter. This experiment was done. Discovering what she wanted in a sexual partner wasn't going to happen here. She needed something real. Someone real.

"I don't think I believe you. See, he didn't just say to put him on the list. He said he was to be the only one on the list."

That shouldn't be hot, right? "Uhm okay."

"You're going to be here and dance for him." Clean's words didn't seem to be a question, but she nodded. His chuckle held no warmth. "Good. He said to tell you that you're a spy and he is the mark."

It took a minute for her to realize Tek had requested a specific roleplay. One which sounded like a lot of fun. "Sounds good."

Clean nodded and patted her knee. "Have fun and this club will miss you."

"Th-Thanks." Her nerves danced in her stomach. Was she making a mistake dancing for a man who had run away from her?

The heavy base of the strip club's music beat against Tek's exhausted brain. He had stopped at the bar in Darklights before heading back to confront the woman he had let fool him. This was the first time he had ever needed liquid courage to face an enemy. He'd performed many interrogations, both for the military and for his Dark Sons Brothers. None of his experience would help him here. He didn't think he could physically hurt her. If it came to that, he would have to call in Clean.

His Brother might not be an officer, but his role within the Club was well defined. He cleaned up messes of an inconvenient nature, and he did it without any blowback. Clean's past before the Dark Sons' Road Captain, Max had nominated him for membership was a mystery.

It was rumored Clean had been part of operations so black no one alive knew the details. What Tek understood was he was the one you called when you needed information and didn't want the body of the source of intel ever found.

He signaled the bartender to give him a double of his usual scotch. Drinking on zero sleep and minimal food was not smart, but if he was to follow through with his plan, it was necessary. He sipped the twenty-five-year-old liquor, trying to flesh out his plan.

"Another one bites the dust. First Sharp, then Dragon, guess you are the next fool to fall." Clean leaned against the bar at Tek's shoulder.

"It's not like that." Tek took the last sip of his drink.

"You get one private dance then call us demanding she dance only for you. I find out she's planning on quitting. Wasn't even going to do the private tonight till she found out it was you. So yeah, I think it's exactly like that."

"She's not who you think she is."

Clean raised an eyebrow. "She's not a millionaire shut-in who is getting her kicks by taking her clothes off for what she probably considers pocket change?"

"You knew?" Tek was pissed. He was the intelligence guy for the Dark Sons. How was it he knew so little about this woman?

"I do my homework on all the girls here. I make sure I am familiar with all their problems so they don't blow back on the club. Had her followed. Every night she takes her way too expensive car and drops her earnings at some women's shelter before heading home to her exclusive condo in a private development."

"Why didn't you tell me?"

"I did. Told you the girl on stage wasn't real."

Tek clenched his fist around the empty glass. "Did you know she's a hacker? Who moved into a condo, which happens to be next to my top encryption specialist? That only a few months later some of my customers get hacked. Hacked so well, we don't even figure it out for almost a year. Then she gets a job here and at my company. Did you know that?"

Clean's face lost all expression. "You saying she's been playing us all?"

"I'm saying one coincidence might be chance, but this many is too much."

Clean leaned forward on his elbow, shaking his head. "I don't know, man. If this is all an act, she deserves all the fucking Oscars."

"Can't risk it." Tek rubbed his eyes. It had been a long two days. He didn't like the idea of her being involved either, but this wasn't a small thing that could be overlooked.

"What's the play? Max is the only other Brother here tonight." Tek could see Clean still had reservations, but like a loyal Brother he would back him up.

"Going to ask her some questions and get the answers I need."

"Fuck, Brother. We are not set up for that kinda shit here. Walls are thin by design. Witnesses everywhere. If this goes sideways, I don't think even I could clean that mess up."

"She's soft. I can break her with mind games alone."

"And if you can't?"

Tek took a deep breath, gathering all his emotions and shoving them in a mental box. "Then we relocate and I let you do your thing."

Chapter 16

It's all fun and games till—

Angela stood outside the private dance room and let herself slip into her role. She was Cami, a Russian spy sent in to seduce the wealthy American businessman. She wore a silky black nightgown with a matching robe that she had intended to be a costume for when she did a film noir routine.

She opened the door without knocking, her best sultry smile on her face, and had to pause as she took in Tek. He was still wearing the suit he had been in yesterday. His hair was rumpled and it looked like he had endured a bad day. Despite all of that, the dark heat in his gray eyes made things tingle low in her body.

It made her feel special that he had obviously had a long, hard day, but had still come to spend time with her.

"You look as if you had a hard day, darlink." She almost

winced at how bad her Russian accent was but held it together wanting to give this gorgeous man his fantasy.

"You have no idea." Tek's growled words vibrated in her chest.

She stepped inside the room and was surprised to see they were alone. No bouncer and the curtains were drawn over the observation windows. Only the little red light on the camera in the corner gave any indication that someone might be watching to keep her safe.

She had planned to send the bouncer out of the room, but the change, without her consent, made her nervous. This wasn't a stranger though, so she didn't let herself worry.

"Sit down, let me give you a massage and you can tell me about your day."

Tek unbuttoned the top half of his shirt, shaking his head. Cami enjoyed the smooth muscled chest that was exposed. "I don't want to talk about it."

Remembering her role, she slipped off the robe and moved closer, rubbing her hands along his chest. She pouted and rubbed her body against his. The growing evidence of his arousal pressed against her stomach. "But you know how much I love hearing about your important job and all those powerful people."

Her lines could use work but Tek hadn't given her much notice or information to work with. Playing the seductress was definitely fun. She felt his fist clench in her hair, the tiny pain as he pulled her head backwards exciting. "I think we should talk about your day. What have you been up to?"

His question was whispered against her lips causing her whole-body to shudder. "Nothing. I was lonely waiting for you to come home."

The whole world seemed to tip sideways in an instant. One minute she was standing pressed against him, the next she was on her back on the couch. His body pressed against hers. His hands trapping hers above her head. She felt her shoes slip off, then heard the clicks as they hit the floor.

Everything was so intense her breath came in quick pants as he took her mouth like he had been starving for her taste. Cami groaned, writhing against him, his cock pressed the satin of her underwear deliciously against her clit. Warm fur engulfed her wrists and two tiny snicks echoed through the room.

Cuffs? Her brain barely registered the thought before he dropped one hand to her breast and started pinching and twisting the bud. Electric pleasure shot straight to her core and she thrust upward trying to chase the orgasm she knew was coming. Right as she was about to fall over the edge, Tek lifted up. The aborted orgasm was almost painful.

"No!" Her denial was a hoarse moan.

She felt herself dragged off the couch by her wrists into a standing position, a few quick steps and the cold metal of the stripper pole startled her as she was pressed against it. Before she could mentally catch up, she stood with her wrists chained to the ceiling and an almost feral man in front of her, dragging in breaths, as he examined her helpless position.

Tek produced a knife from somewhere and exquisite fear sent chills down her spine. Her voice and breath caught as he slid the metal along her collarbone. Quick flicks sent the material of her nightgown pooling to the floor leaving her in only a thong.

The tip of the knife scraped between her breasts, down her stomach, to her hip where he removed that last piece of clothing. Cami had never considered knife play in her many fantasies but knew now it would take a starring role.

Tek tossed the knife onto the couch and ran his hands down her bare sides. He leaned in and whispered into her ear, "You want me to make you come?"

His fingers traced the wetness leaking down her thigh up to her aching cunt. "Please. Yes."

His fingers filled her and she couldn't help but cry out in pleasure. He stroked the spot deep inside her that caused a new more intense orgasm to start building in her core.

"If you want to come, you have to tell me what I want to know."

Okay they were flipping the script. She could go with that. "Anything. I'll tell you whatever you want."

Tek's thumb circled her clit with maddening slow strokes. "Good girl. Did you steal information from my company?"

His other hand brushed against her nipple making thought almost impossible. Yes or no what was the answer that would get her what she wanted. If she said yes maybe he would spank her. But she was supposed to be a hardened spy shouldn't she resist more?

Tek stopped his motions and her body jerked in protest.

"Answer me." He spoke his command directly against her throat his teeth nipping at the sensitive skin there.

"Yes!"

His thumb moved in a brutal swipe across her clit and she felt tears as they started to run down her cheeks in frustration. She almost feared the intensity of the upcoming orgasm. That it would steal her sanity.

"You hacked my company and stole confidential information." His fingers began slowly thrusting again. "What's your handle, little hacker? What's the name you sign on all your crimes?"

He felt so good stretching her with his fingers. Creativity was washed away by her body's need to find release. So she gave him a small piece of reality. "C A - 1 0 0 0 0 0 0."

He paused and gave her a puzzled look. The endorphins running through her body had her giggling at his confusion.

"CA-million. Chameleon, get it?" She giggled again at his scowl.

He stepped back and the loss of his heat made her whine.

"You think this is funny, Angela? You might have destroyed hundreds of lives. My company might not survive." Tek turned his back on her pacing the short length of the room.

Her name was like ice water spilled down her spine. What was he talking about? They were just playing a game. Weren't they?

Chapter 17

Assumptions make an ass out of you, not me.

Tek paced, trying to get his body under control. She really was the perfect honeypot. Her body, her mind, all of it, the perfect bait to catch him. Hell, if they hadn't caught the hack when they did, she would have had him wrapped around her little finger in days.

Two more questions, then he would never have to see her again. The thought shouldn't have bothered him, but it did. He turned, taking in her curvy perfection. Hands tied above her head, she was his every fantasy in one devious package.

"T-Tek, what are y-you talking about?" He didn't like how small her voice sounded. His conscience pricked at him, but he pushed it down.

He stepped forward and she reared back in fright, kicking out at him. Good, she should be scared. He batted her legs down and closed a hand around her throat. He squeezed with the lightest of pressure, letting her feel what he could do if he chose to. Her pupils were wide as he held her gaze.

"Two more questions. How did you bypass the encryption and who did you give the information to?"

Angela shook her head, her purple locks brushing her shoulders. "I d-don't want to do this anymore. This roleplay is over. L-let me go."

He grabbed her chin, trying to ignore the tears streaming out of her eyes. She was an actress playing him and it wouldn't work. "No, CA-million." He spit out the hacker name like it left a nasty taste in his mouth. "Not a game. These are actual people you've hurt and there will be real consequences."

The tears seemed to dry up. Her eyes were wide, beautiful, shimmering teal. "Y-you think I hacked your company. You did all of this…" She drew in a deep breath, her eyes now glittering with anger. *"SASAFRASS!! HELP!"*

The lights began to strobe, and the door popped open. Tek didn't understand what was going on.

"Stop all activity. Security is on its way." A loud siren followed the recorded male voice.

A half-dressed girl popped her head in the door, horror filling her face.

"Run, Jasmine, get help!" Angela's screamed words were barely understandable over the racket, but the girl dashed away before Tek could react.

Decaf ran in the room and froze, obviously not sure what to do. "Everything okay?"

Clean was right behind him, opening a panel near the door and typing in a code that caused all the noise and strobing lights to stop. The silence and bright glow made the scene almost unreal.

"What the fuck was that?" Tek snarled, pissed his plan had turned into a circus.

"Decaf, go calm everyone down. Tell them I've got this under control." When the Prospect left the room, Clean closed the door. "That is a safe word system I put in for the girls' safety."

"Don't you think you should have mentioned it?"

"Is he i-in on your s-sicko plan to use sex to get me to admit to crimes I-I didn't commit?"

"Don't bullshit us. You admitted to hacking my company."

Angela gave a frustrated scream and looked over at Clean. "I was t-told I was to be a spy, and you were my mark. It was r-roleplaying!"

Pain pounded Tek's temples. Lack of sleep and food was catching up with him. When he had told Clean to tell her that, he thought it would help with the mind-fuck not muddy the waters.

"C-Clean." Angela's voice had lost all inflection. The hollow sound hurt something inside of Tek. "If you get me down now and let me go, I won't call the cops. You will never have to see or hear from me again. But if one more thing happens to me before then, I will bring legal hell down on you all."

Tek was confused by Angela's confidence. She sounded more like a robot than a woman, all her nerves and stuttering gone. "What makes you think you'll be able to call the cops?" He didn't understand why he was pushing her. Maybe he hoped to spark some fire back into her eyes.

She looked back at him with empty eyes. "Do you know what dead man's files are, Tek? Clean does."

Her question sent a chill down Tek's spine. "Blackmail material, timed to go public if you don't stop it."

She nodded. "My father was a genius, but paranoid. He taught me to keep a list of people most likely to kill me and keep their info in those files."

Tek glanced over at his friend and didn't like the ice that had seemed to fill his eyes. "So?"

A tear glistened as it ran down her cheek as she looked at Clean. "The things they m-made you do in the name of Country were wrong. And I'm s-sorry. Operation Little Phoenix is in those files along with the fact you are alive, your c-code name, and current location." Visible tremors shook Clean's body at her words. "I d-did wipe all traces of your birth identity from every classified and non-classified s-server I had access to. The scholarships your n-niece and n-nephew won should pay for any school they want to go to. I also paid off all your parents' debts."

"That was you?" The wonder in Clean's voice was out of character.

"Unlike Uncle Sam, I believe our heroes and their families deserve to be taken care of. I also know that using a stick instead of a carrot should only be a last resort."

Clean reached up as if to let her go and Tek grabbed his Brother by the arm. "What the fuck are you doing?"

"We have a hallway full of witnesses. What the fuck do you think are our options?"

The door opened and Max walked in. Max was the Dark Sons' Road Captain and usually one of the most laid-back of Tek's Brothers. The look on his face now said anything but chill. He grabbed the black silk robe off the floor and before anyone could say anything had Angela out of the cuffs and into her robe.

Tek went to protest, but Max's raised hand silenced him. Everything was going sideways. Why not one more complication? Max leaned down, looking Angela in the eyes. "I've been watching the feed. Heard what you offered. You go, no retribution. We got a deal, Ms. Turner?"

Angela blinked a few times as if she was trying to focus. "Jeffrey?"

Who the hell was Jeffrey?

His Brother shook his head, his lips pulled tight. "Name's Max. Do we have a deal?"

She nodded. "Yeah. I'm not an idiot, Max. No r-retribution. You never have to see me again." She pulled the robe tightly around her and scurried from the room.

Tek couldn't take it anymore, he screamed and punched the wall, not registering the pain.

"That's the girl, Clean said, you think hacked your company?" Max's steady voice did little to calm Tek down.

"Yeah, and you let her get away." Tek gestured at the door.

Max crossed his arms. "You got evidence?"

"Yeah. I had monitoring software on her terminal. It caught her poking around in the breached databases today."

Max snorted. "Then it wasn't her."

Clean tilted his head. "Not exactly making sense, Max. She has the skills, the opportunity, and Tek caught her red-handed. I admit, I don't like her for it either, but you seem sure."

"If she was hacking your company, you wouldn't know about it until the Feds were banging down your door with enough evidence to put you away for life." Max leaned against the wall, reached up, and pulled the plug from the security camera.

Tek growled, frustrated at not knowing what was going on. He was used to having more information than anyone else in the room. But these two Brothers had backgrounds so black it was surprising they could even handle sunlight.

He tried to get his swerving emotions under control. He needed to take a step back and look at the situation with unemotional logic. If they were right, he had just abused a woman who didn't deserve it. Shame threatened to bubble up, but he pushed it down.

"What do you know?" Tek kept his voice cool.

Max leaned against the wall, tilting his head up at the ceiling. "Fourteen years ago, a white-hat hacker named CA-million exposed a pyramid scheme that was stealing money from the elderly. That was her first big act. More followed, all with the same MO. Someone was hurting someone else, and evidence would appear to make it stop. She would have stayed anonymous if she hadn't made friends with the wrong hacker who sold her out for a reduced sentence." He sighed. "I was part of the team sent to bring her in. Fuck, she was a kid, and the government threatened her and her father if she didn't start working for them."

"So she works for the government?" Clean asked.

"Nope." Max chuckled. "She smiled and said they could start negotiations in a week. Five days later we were told to release her. No explanations, nothing. Now, officially, I don't know shit. I do know that a few times a year CA-million sends actionable intel that saves lives to authorities. Angela Turner never has worked directly for the government, though they have offered her anything she wants. The closest she has come to working for them is consulting through a third party and giving them first rights to purchase her work. Those programs now make up the backbone of our security for the intelligence networks."

Tek tried to take in everything Max's words meant. She was so much more than he had ever imagined. Brilliant, beautiful, and could probably have solved all of his problems. But he had let paranoia and fear of his attraction to her push him into actions that made him her enemy.

How the fuck was he going to fix this?

Chapter 18

Pronouns are confusing. I mean, can a noun really get paid?

A ngela embraced the pain in her hands as she pounded on Jojo's door. Her life was spiraling apart, and she needed her friend to hold her together. Joshua opened the door, tired and slightly rumpled, wearing a navy-blue nightgown and robe which reminded her too much of the outfit she'd worn for Tek earlier.

She couldn't control the sob that exploded out of her. Joshua pulled her inside and into his arms, closing the door behind them. "Oh, sweetie. What's wrong?"

Angela couldn't stop her tears. "I-I need you to put on your w-wig. I need Jojo."

"Oh, honey-child, I don't need my fabulous and expensive hair to give you that." The now sultry, southern, feminine tone of his voice brought her some comfort.

"But I need my girlfriend and the internet says it is respectful to use the right pronouns." The logic puzzle that was working out her friend's fluid gender was helping to calm her down.

Jojo rolled her eyes and pulled her forward into the living room. "They are my pronouns and, sure as rain in April, I will use them as I see fit. Woman. Man. I am both and neither, so if you need a girlfriend right now, that is who I am. The internet can mind its own business."

Jojo sat down and Angela cuddled into her side, letting all the confusion wash over her in a flood of tears. When her sobs had become hiccups, her friend rubbed her back in soothing circles.

"You ready to tell me what has you all riled up?"

The day had been filled with so many bad things it was hard to pick where to start. Beginning with the most painful would be confusing. Chronologically seemed best.

"R-Rick sent me home early and threatened to f-fire me." The taste of bile filled her mouth at the memory of his smug face and hurtful words.

"What reason would that pompous windbag have to fire you?" Jojo pulled back for a moment and got an excited look on her face. "Did you hit him in the nuts?"

Angela laughed and felt some of her tension flowing out of her. "No. Though it was tempting. I insulted the GUI code and apparently it's his private domain."

"Only Rick is allowed to insult code?"

"No, apparently the GUI code is his baby. I know no one enjoys hearing their baby is ugly, but I'm telling you, Jojo, this crap was nightmare inducing."

She raised a well plucked eyebrow. "Isn't all GUI code bad?"

"Not like this. It was full of hidden routines and custom crap that not only slowed everything down, but actually bypassed encryption in others. I only parsed through maybe half of it, but there is no way it is worth fixing. Starting from scratch would be better and faster."

"Hold up there. Did you just say the GUI bypasses encryption?"

"Yeah, I know this program is still in Beta, but I don't care how annoying it is to enter passwords, you shouldn't put hacks like that into code. What if you forgot to pull them before the program went live? It is amateur hour."

"Which program were you working on?" Jojo's voice lost its teasing tone.

"I tried to text you and ask what to do, but you said you were swamped."

"I'm not mad at you, darlin, and I shouldn't even be telling you this much, but we had a major hack happen yesterday that had most of us stumped."

"Yeah, no breaking news there. Tek thinks I did it."

"Tek?"

"Oh, sorry. Mr. Vallier came to Darklights and interrogated me."

"Damn that fool." Jojo huffed. "He had the nerve to accuse me of sharing classified information with you."

"But you didn't! You aren't in trouble, are you?" Angela couldn't stand it if she caused any harm in Jojo's life. She would do anything necessary to fix things for her friend who was now a vital pillar within her life.

"I best not be," Jojo snapped dramatically above her head. "But I told that man he didn't have the sense God gave little apples if he thought you were behind the hack."

Jojo's support felt almost as good as Tek's betrayal had hurt. More tears leaked out of her eyes as she remembered how he had turned something so amazing into nothing more than a dirty trick. Her mind relived the amazing moment right before it all fell apart. *And he didn't even let me come!*

Angela's body was a rollercoaster of conflicting sensations.

She ached to feel him inside her, her stomach boiled with nerves and distrust, and her head pounded from thinking of how her friend might lose her job.

Jojo burst out laughing, wiping nonexistent tears from her eyes. "Who exactly didn't let you come?"

"I said that out loud?" Heat flushed her cheeks.

"Oh, you definitely did. Though I'm crossing my fingers and toes that, *him*, isn't who I think it is. Didn't we discuss earlier what an epically bad idea hooking your wagon to that man was?"

"Not my fault, he came after me!" Angela's shoulders dropped. "And there will be no wagon hooking."

Jojo spread her arms and motioned for Angela to snuggle in close. She did, loving the comfort she found in her muscular arms.

"Now tell Jojo all about it. I need context and details if I'm going to help you plot proper revenge."

She shook her head. "Can't do revenge. I promised."

"Well, I didn't. So spill."

Angela gave her friend the story, not sparing herself any embarrassment. The only thing she left out was what Clean's secret was. By the time she was done, both of them were tense and shaking.

Jojo's breath shook as she spoke. "He tried to interrogate you like a two-bit spy in a bad porno movie?"

Angela's chuckle was dry. "I wouldn't call it a bad porno movie, but yes."

Jojo scowled. "How good his bedroom skills are is not the point. If the club hadn't had that safe word thingy he wasn't planning on stopping."

"I don't think he would have kept up the sex stuff." Was she being naïve? She hadn't believed he was capable of doing what he did. No. She had to believe he would have stopped anything physical. "We seemed to have moved on to the threats portion of the interrogation."

"And he knew you are a virgin?" Jojo's face got all serious. "You are still a virgin, right?"

Would she still be a virgin if things hadn't taken a turn for the weird? Probably not. "Yes, and unfortunately, yes."

"Good. Did you tell him what you found in the GUI?"

Crap. She had meant to tell Tek the next time she saw him. But then he had asked for the spy thing, and she had forgotten all about it. "No. It didn't seem important at the time."

"That's where you're wrong." Jojo sat up and moved so they were facing each other and took her hands. "Let me guess, you were working on GX2 project."

Wow. Vallier had to have lots of software she could have been working on. How was Jojo so certain? "Yeah."

"Well, the framework for GX2 was pulled from the original GX platform and is being used for a new super-secret project. The differences are only on the backend. So I'm guessing you found the answer to the mystery we have all been banging our heads against."

Horror filled her at the thought that what she had seen was in use. "You mean that code is out in the field? There are people actually using it!"

"Yes." Her friend squeezed her hands. "It is tempting to let that asshole swing in the wind. But I know you don't have that in you."

"No, I can't work there anymore, but I have to let them know what Rick's negligence leaves them open to."

"Okay, so here is what we are going to do…"

Chapter 19

There isn't a box of chocolates big enough to fix this mess.

"What the fuck did you do?" Lisen's shout preceded her into Tek's office.

Her loud shout set off a drumline inside his head. It was eight-thirty in the morning and the Scotch Tek used the previous night to get some sleep was still in his system. He managed a few hours of rest, and his dreams, and the clarity rest brought, told him one thing. He'd fucked up.

How was he going to fix this? Would she come after him financially? The news was full of women who sued for things much less damming than he had done. She deserved whatever she asked for, but money wouldn't buy her silence, especially if she believed he was a danger to others. He had given her no reason not to think the worst of him.

Exhaustion and stress were no excuse. But if he was honest, he wanted more than her silence. He wanted forgiveness. Actually, he wanted to erase the last twenty-four hours and go back to when there was a slight chance of him becoming something special to her.

Lisen slammed her palms onto his desk, snapping him back into the moment. "Are you listening to me?"

"The entire floor heard you." Tek rubbed his eyes. "But you're going to need to be more specific."

Whatever had crawled up Lisen's ass couldn't be half as important as figuring out how to convince Angela to help them out in solving the current crisis. Maybe if they could work together, she would see what he'd done was a desperate move by someone who cared deeply for his company and its employees.

"How about this? Why is Jojo downstairs in her full-on Scary Spice outfit?"

He did not know what a Scary Spice outfit was or why one of his employees wearing one was a problem. "I don't know. And why do you care what she is wearing?"

"I care because she strutted into my office with your gal pal at her side. Slammed down both of their resignations and told me I had twenty minutes to meet them in the conference room with HR or she wouldn't bother to tell me how to fix the hack."

"Wait, what?" Tek stood, trying to make sense of everything. His stomach lurched. Angela quitting shouldn't be a surprise, but for some reason it hadn't occurred to him. In all his plans, from the ridiculous to the practical, he had thought she would stay.

Crap, had she told her friend what he had done? If it got around, he was finished. Tek knew he deserved whatever followed. He just thought he would have more than a few hours to plan.

He could step down, let Kane and Lisen rebrand. That might be enough to make sure his life's work didn't go up in flames. It hit him. They had figured out the hack and were going to tell Lisen. It was good news, great even, but it meant he would no longer have any excuse for talking to Angela.

"Holy shit, Tek. How bad is this?" His face probably reflected his thoughts because his unflappable CIO was looking pale.

He was tempted to blow things off and pray he was wrong about why they were demanding HR, but Tek had never been a coward.

"Best case, a large cash settlement and an NDA. Worst case, I'll step down and you and Kane will have to pick up the pieces."

Lisen sat down in the chair across from his desk with a stiffness that broadcast her anger loud and clear. "I need more than that."

"I questioned her last night and things got out of hand."

Through a tight jaw, Lisen asked, "You assaulted her?"

"No!" Tek ran a hand through his hair. "Not exactly. I…" He huffed out a breath and gave Lisen an abridged version of what happened minus any details about his Brothers.

Lisen held her fists so tight the knuckles were white. "We have two minutes to get down to HR. We are not done talking. Not by a long shot."

Lisen stood and strode out of the room without looking back. Outside of his Brothers, Lisen and Kane were the most important people in his life. Lisen lived and worshipped at the altar of safe, sane, and consensual. Even with all their history, he didn't know if she would forgive him for breaking the cardinal rule of BDSM by trying to steal a submissive's choice.

His fuck up may have cost him more than even he could afford to pay.

Chapter 20

Forgive and Forget? I'm neither Jesus nor do I have Alzheimers.

"Explain to me again, Jojo, why you look like an escapee of the London punk movement and I'm dressed up like a Japanese anime schoolgirl?" Angela pulled down on her short, pleated skirt.

They were sitting alone at a long table in the same conference room where two days ago she had attended orientation. Lisen was off getting HR per Jojo's demands. The two of them had stayed up most of the night gathering the evidence to prove what was wrong with the software and a proposal for both the quickest and the best way to fix it. Then Jojo had woken her up and spent over an hour fussing with Angela's appearance, calling it armoring up for battle.

"Two reasons. One." Jojo held up a finger for emphasis. "You need girl power. No stuttering or hesitation. You are Cami or CA-million, undercover superhero, right out of a movie. You are here to save all their asses, even though you owe them *N-O-T-H-I-N-G!*"

Okay. That was a good idea. Roleplaying would help her get through this with strength and dignity, even if *he* showed up. "Right, but why the schoolgirl outfit?"

Jojo held up a second finger. "Two. I am fabulous in leopard print and you are every geek boy's fantasy. Even if said boy pretends they're a billionaire biker bad boy. If he dares show his face, he will immediately regret losing a chance at the fabulousness that is you."

How had she gotten so lucky as to have a great friend like Jojo? "It's not too late to take back your resignation. I know how much you loved working here. I don't want you to be out of work because of me."

"Please, honey child, I have the numbers of several recruiters who have been begging me to jump ship. This magnificent mind will not be sitting idle for any longer than I take to pick up the phone. Besides, I'm saving myself the legal fees I'd incur if I stayed here after beating that man to a bloody pulp."

She giggled, trying to picture the two fighting. Jojo was tough, but she wouldn't stand a chance against the much more muscular and well-trained Tek. Her laughter faded as she realized she would probably never see him again.

Angela's self-confidence had taken a hit by what he had done, but her body still longed to find out what he would be like in bed. His deep voice telling her all the dirty things he wanted to do. She wanted his dominance in the bedroom and his challenging, brilliant mind outside of it.

The door to the room opened and Angela's breath caught as four people walked in. Lisen was in the lead, followed by a man and woman she didn't recognize. Tek was last into the room. He looked tired, but somehow still as commanding as ever. His gray eyes locked onto her and Angela felt her knees weaken.

No. She was a badass superhero, not a whimpering pushover. She would give them her evidence and leave. She took a deep breath and enjoyed how Tek's gaze heated. Jojo was right, she was every geek's fantasy. And if she had to walk away, she was going to give him a memory to remember her by.

Using her best ice princess voice, she addressed the room. "Let's get this over with."

The four sat down on the other side of the table as if readying for battle. HR being present was Jojo's idea, wanting Tek to sweat that Angela was going to file harassment charges. She doubted a man like him worried about those things, but she had wanted witnesses so their information didn't get ignored. Angela leaned down and pulled a file folder and a USB drive out of the messenger bag that acted as her purse.

She slid both across the table to Lisen. Jojo leaned back in her chair, crossing her arms and glaring at Tek. Lisen opened the file and her brow furrowed at the highlighted printouts.

Angela cleared her throat. "What you are looking at is the code for the GX and GX2 GUI interface. The yellow highlighted portions are vulnerable to any moderately talented hacker, though your excellent encryption would block them from obtaining anything of value."

"Why thank you, honey." Jojo smiled, breaking off her glaring for a moment.

"Nothing but truth."

Lisen flipped through the pages and looked up. "And the pink highlights?"

Angela leaned forward, doing her best to ignore Tek's intense stare. "That is what screwed you. If you know where to click and what to type, you can access anything in the databases without credentials. At first I thought this was just sloppy work of someone too lazy to bother with logins. I was wrong."

"You're saying someone did this on purpose?" Tek's almost whispered voice rattled her calm.

"Yes. But I want to make something very clear." Angela gave everyone at the table a stern glare. "That information along with everything on the drive was dropped off anonymously. If asked, you are to say, you do not know where it came from."

"Why?" Lisen asked at the same time Tek asked, "Or?"

Angela sighed. It was time to show them both the carrot and stick.

"Why doesn't matter. The or is this, last night I recovered the security footage from Darklights you deleted. If you tell anyone the files came from me, I will release it, along with enough damning information to lose you almost every client you have."

"What's on the drive?" Angela was impressed, Tek's face showed no reaction, though his voice was tight.

"Information retrieved from one of your employee's personal phones. Emails proving, he sold customer information. Off-shore accounts with corresponding payments. The USB also contains everything I could find on who checked the code in without review and trace backs to the workstation IP." Angela shook her head. "If you're going to commit a crime, you shouldn't use your personal phone that backs up to a barely secure cloud service."

When they found that information last night, it had shocked her and Jojo both. Hacking Rick's info had been a hunch after she had seen that most of the damaging code was added or altered after the system went live.

"I hope that asshole ends up someone's bitch in jail." Jojo's comment startled a laugh out of her.

Lisen picked up the USB. "Let me guess, it's encrypted,

and you'll give us the key to this illegally obtained information for some sum of money."

"Oh honey," Jojo responded before she could deny anything. "You know I love your claws as much as any Diva would, but you got my girl all wrong."

"Then what does she want?"

Jojo stood up on her platform heels and leaned forward on the table. "Nothing. She wants nothing." The drag queen turned her glare on Tek. "What she deserves is for pretty-boy over there to admit he is lower than a set of snake's testicles. You all should be on your knees thanking Baby Jesus the goddess that is my girl isn't a vengeful bitch like me."

Angela cut in before Jojo could say anymore. "The data isn't encrypted. I'll make it easy for you, the person screwing your company is Richard Nelson."

Lisen sat back as if stunned. Tek cursed and pulled out his cellphone hitting a few keys.

"Kane, have Rick Nelson brought to my office and make sure he doesn't leave."

Everyone on the other side of the table had their phones out and were typing furiously. It was time for her and Jojo to leave. Angela caught her friend's eye, and they both nodded and stood.

"You will find my suggestions on solutions to your problem at the back of the file." Angela turned, ready to move on.

The clack of something metallic hitting the conference table with force had her steps pausing. She looked back and was caught by Tek's steady gaze. He was standing leaning forward, his breaths coming in a deep steady rhythm.

"Can I have a moment alone with Miss Turner?"

"No," Lisen and Jojo said together.

The HR people ignored the negative, stood and scurried towards the door. This little scene was probably more than they had ever bargained for.

Angela studied Tek's face and posture. Tight shoulders and hands, wide gray eyes that had slight bruising under them. He was a mixture of angry, tired, and somehow pleading, though she knew he would never do that.

"It's fine, Jojo." When her friend crossed her arms with a stubborn glare, Angela sighed. "You can stand outside the glass and make sure he doesn't do anything."

Jojo scowled and placed a hand on her shoulder. "You don't have to be alone with him if you don't want to be."

"It's okay. He can't hurt me anymore." Tek flinched at the words Angela knew to be a lie. For some reason she still wanted him, which meant he still had some power over her. She also knew if she didn't talk to him this one last time, she would regret it. Always wonder what he would have said.

"If you're sure." At her nod, Jojo gestured to Lisen. "Come on Ice Queen, lets watch your boy from the other side of the glass door."

Lisen stood up with fire in her eyes. "If he was my boy, he'd be gagged in the corner with a welted ass."

"Lisen," Tek growled.

She put her hands up in mock defeat. "Going, Boss."

Angela played nervously with the edge of her pleated skirt, waiting for Tek to say something. The silence in the room grew heavy. Lisen and Jojo stood right outside the door, obviously not planning on going anywhere.

"I'm sorry." Tek's sudden words startled her. He stood and turned his back to her to gaze out the windows that lined the wall.

His words were a tiny balm, but not nearly enough. She waited for him to say more, but the silence continued to wrap around them. Almost two minutes passed before he placed a hand on the window and spoke.

"This company was supposed to change the world. Find the lost, protect the innocent, do right in this fucked up place we call home. Instead, we protect money and corporations. Clean up after a government which can't or won't keep its own people safe."

Angela's heart ached for the agony she heard in his voice. She understood his pain. The guilt of not being able to do enough, no matter how hard you tried. It was what had driven her every day right up until the moment her father died. The programs she wrote, the systems she hacked, were her way of using her mind to make the world a better place.

She spoke the truth and gave him what comfort she could. "This company has saved lives. I wouldn't have come to work at your company if it hadn't."

A small thump startled her as he banged his fist against the glass. "It's not enough."

Angela walked over to stand next to the man who had captured her every fantasy. They made a strange pair reflected in the glass. His clean-cut corporate look contrasted with her purple hair and strange schoolgirl outfit. On the outside he represented the supposed right path in life, and she the twisty back roads. It just went to show that packaging didn't match the inside truth of a person.

There was no right path in life, only thousands of choices. The important one's rarely had anything to do with conforming to the social norm. Instead, it was the choices to keep moving forward even when the outcome was uncertain or frightening. Not letting the past weigh you down like an anchor and choose instead to learn from it and be better.

"Then do more. If you don't want to protect corporations, sell that part of the company and use the money to do what you do want to do."

Tek chuckled. "You make it sound so easy."

She shrugged. "Nothing worthwhile is easy. Doesn't mean you shouldn't try."

He turned and faced her. He reached out and brushed a stray lock of hair behind her ear. "Can you forgive me?"

"I don't know." Angela brushed a finger down her reflection in the glass. "You took something special that was growing between us and twisted it against me." She took a deep breath and dropped her hand, looking at him through their reflections. "What would you have done if the club hadn't had the safe word system?"

"I lost control last night." Tek rubbed his neck and looked up at the ceiling. "The last few months have been crazy. Then I found out I could lose this company to an enemy I didn't even know I had. I'm not trying to make excuses." He looked down at her. "I saw you had been in the databases that had been compromised and I snapped."

So that was why he had been so sure she was involved. There were a hundred other explanations for her being in those databases. Explanations were nice, but it didn't make his betrayal hurt less. "That doesn't answer the question."

"I've been drawn to you from the moment we met. Even as crazy as I was, I know I couldn't have physically harmed you." His chest rose and fell with a deep breath. "I also don't think I would have let you leave without giving me answers."

Angela wasn't sure if the chill that ran down her spine was from fear or excitement. The truth of his words was apparent in every line of his face. Reality and roleplay could blur lines that shouldn't be crossed. The idea of being held hostage for real did not appeal but as a fantasy... All the more reason she needed to walk away. For the type of relationship she wanted, trust was not only important, it was necessary.

Angela stepped back from the window and nodded. "I don't hate you, Tek. I mourn the loss of trust and what we could have been. But I refuse to give in to my anger and lash out. Not sure if that answers your question any more than you answered mine." Her chest ached knowing it was time to leave. She needed to say one more thing. "I do wish you happiness, whatever that looks like for you."

Angela turned, picked up her bag, and strode out of the conference room. She was proud that she didn't glance back once as her heart cracked at the finality of it all. Jojo walked by her side quietly until they reached the lobby.

"You okay, Cami girl?"

Angela slowed as they walked out the front doors. She needed a moment to sort through her thoughts. Was she okay? Logically, she understood what had happened and why. His methods had been extreme. Unacceptable. But was it unforgivable? Did forgiving him even matter since she never planned to see him again?

"I'm trying to decide if I can forgive him."

"His groveling must have been spectacular. I didn't see any begging on bended knee."

"He apologized. But no begging. I don't think he's wired that way."

"Ugh." Jojo threw her arms into the air, spinning as if shouting to the universe. "My girl is a saint! Everyone gather and witness her halo."

They were about to step off the curb into the parking lot when Angela heard the shrieking tone she had set on her phone for urgent updates, go off.

"Hold up a second." She dug into her bag, trying to remember what program she had running that might be sending her an alert. With a couple clicks she silenced the phone and opened the attachment.

Facial recognition match 94%

Child services file #85327

Phoebe Smith

Angela scanned the file, shocked by what she saw. She had found Tek's sister! The girl had been found alone in an apartment when her supposed mother died of an OD. The woman had been squatting in an abandoned building and had no ID. With nothing to go on, the police didn't bother looking any further. The traumatized child barely talked so had been given a name and issued a social security number and been dropped into the child welfare system. Picture after picture as she aged matched the projections Angela's program had created almost perfectly.

"I have to go back inside."

Jojo gave her a skeptical look. "Why?"

The bang of a sliding car door caught Angela's attention. Two men dressed in black military fatigues jumped out of a white van parked not fifteen feet away. Chills ran down her spine at their hard expressions and cold eyes as they focused on her. What the hell? Why were men in masks coming for her? Just as the impulse to run hit her muscles, one of them grabbed her roughly by the arm.

Fuck!

Chapter 21

Being a woman means being able to kick ass in heels and a killer outfit.

Tek had intended to get in the elevator and head up to his office to untangle the mess that Rick had made of his company and life. When he stepped onto the elevator, he hadn't been able to suppress the urge to see Angela one more time and pressed the button for the lobby. He just barely caught sight of Angela's purple hair as she and Jojo walked out the front doors. He wanted to stop her, call her back and demand she give him another chance, but he didn't.

He stopped at the front security desk and felt like a creeper watching the two friends talk and pause near the parking lot. Her words echoed in his head. 'I do wish you happiness, whatever that looks like for you.' Even after everything he had done, she still was kind to him. What did happiness look like?

Since the day his sister disappeared, he had done everything in his power to fill the void left by his giggling angel. First, with the military, then with the Dark Sons, and most especially with this company. But it had never been enough. Giving up on personally searching for her six years ago had been a breaking point. After that he had changed the focus of the company towards making money, though he had satisfied his guilt with the small amount of charity work they did. He hadn't given up completely, he still paid an exorbitant amount of money every year to several PI firms to keep the search going but his focus had turned on making this place bigger, better, more profitable.

Why do moments of epiphany always seem to hit you too late to do any good? He had given up on happiness when he had given up on his sister. His Brothers had kept him anchored, their goals giving him purpose. But instead of continuing to search for what he wanted and making a difference, he now ruthlessly chased money like it could solve every problem. That time was over. He would spend the next few days cleaning up the current mess, then find some way to get what he wanted. And he wanted Angela.

An alarm started blinking on the security desk in front of him.

"What is that?" Tek demanded. The seated security personnel were already typing and looking around at their monitors.

"Front gate panic alarm. I don't see Chris on the monitor," the first one said.

"He's not responding to the phone. Roving team three is closest and heading in for a visual," the second added.

Tek was running before he even realized he needed to move. Angela was outside. He needed her safe. Even if this was nothing, it wasn't worth the risk. Tek looked back to the security desk and shouted. "Emergency Protocols! Lock this place down!"

His security staff was all ex-military. Selected and trained by Kane personally, he knew right now they would work to assess the problem. Any of the trained operatives who were in the building would be arming up and heading down to assist in any way they could.

He hit the front doors at a run scanning the area for a flash of purple hair. People milled outside all unaware there might be danger. "Get inside! Emergency protocols! This is not a drill!" he bellowed in his best battlefield voice. "Head to your safe zone, follow the instruction of the security personnel!"

Most people listened, but a few down by the parking lot weren't moving. The outrageous leopard print jumpsuit Jojo had been wearing caught Tek's eye, Angela next to her. A white van stopped in front of them and his pulse jumped. He sprinted in their direction.

Two men jumped out of the cargo door and tried to drag the two women towards the vehicle. Adrenaline spiked in his chest and his speed picked up. His heart beat in his ears, he knew he wouldn't get to them in time.

Jojo punched the man trying to grab her in the throat and caused him to fall back. Terror was a bitter taste in his mouth when Angela dropped as if unconscious. Her attacker wasn't ready for that and she slipped out of his grasp. If she was injured, he would make sure these men suffered.

Two more men jumped from the van to back-up their friends as Jojo somehow managed a beautiful sidekick in her platform heels to the head of the man trying to scoop Angela off the ground. The kidnapper stumbled and dropped his intended victim.

Tek barreled into the man now trying to pick up Angela knocking him away. His opponent reached for a gun and Tek knocked the weapon out of his hand. These were not just random goons. Now, with the surprise of resistance gone, they were starting to coordinate their actions. Tek wanted to check on Angela, but a blow to his shoulder from the man he was fighting forced him to stay focused.

The explosion of a gunshot sounded from nearby. One of the men trying to drag a now struggling Angela into the van fell clutching his leg. Tek connected a blow to his opponent's face. Air rushed out of his lungs from a kick to his own ribs. He circled so his attacker was no longer between him and the women fighting for their freedom. In one fluid motion, he pulled his own gun from the concealed holster at his back and shot the man center mass. The man stumbled back and Tek spun, scanning for the next person to shoot.

Jojo had her attacker in a very elegant sleeper hold. The man's struggles barely moving the large drag queen. Angela must have crawled under the car parked next to her as her attacker was crouched down reaching under it. The man wounded in the knee had pulled himself back into the van. Yards away Kane and three of his operatives were closing quickly on the fight, guns drawn.

The squeal of tires was the only warning Tek got. He dove out of the way of the now moving van. Gunshots filled the air along with the echoing dings as bullet met metal. Tek cursed. The van sped away across the grass to reach the road. The gunshots stopped and he stood slowly trying to fight down the rage and anger flowing through him. The rush of time finally seemed to drift back to normal as Tek looked around.

The man he had shot was clutching his stomach while one of Vallier security stripped him of weapons. The other two men were pressed up against a car as two of Kane's men searched them. A very pissed off Jojo paced behind them. Kane was calling orders through his walkie watching over everything.

Where was Angela?

For a moment Tek's heart seized thinking he had somehow

missed them getting her into the van. A small sob caught his attention. He rushed forward crouching near the car the mercenary had been trying to crawl under. Curled up into a ball under the center of the car was Angela. Air rushed out of his lungs as relief hit him.

"It's all over, kitten. Can you come out of there or do I need to come get you?" The car she was under was low to the ground. Too low for him to fit comfortably. Hopefully, she would come out on her own.

She opened her beautiful teal eyes and looked at him with a fear so strong he could feel it. "T-tek?"

"Yeah, kitten, it's me. Can you come out here?"

"If someone tries to drag you. You should go limp because it is harder to drag dead weight. If they pick you up you should struggle, bite, and scream. If you can, you should run away." A rasping sob shook her body. "I couldn't run away."

He knew she was trying to process what had happened in her own unique way, but it tore him apart. "You did great. You're safe now but you need to come out here so I can hold you." Tek tried to keep his voice calm.

"Statistically, they could have backup."

"Kitten there are a lot of highly trained people out here on our side. You are safe."

Angela muttered to herself for a minute then said clearly. "I want a gun."

Shocked by the request Tek paused for a second. "Do you know how to use a gun?"

"I do. My father thought it was a good skill to know and while I don't currently own a gun, because I thought it overly paranoid and unnecessary, I'm rethinking my position."

He chuckled. "I can understand that. If you come out here, we can see about getting you a gun."

"No. There is only a twenty percent chance of me getting

kidnapped while under this low-riding car. If I go out there without a weapon the odds are too high."

Shaking his head, Tek put the safety on his gun and passed it over to Angela. She unfurled enough to take it from him then, to his surprise, did a quick check of the magazine. He tried not to worry as she slowly crawled out from under the car, the weapon clutched in her hand. She looked so fragile in her tiny schoolgirl uniform, wide teal eyes, and messed purple hair, the handgun an odd fashion statement.

Tek wrapped his arms around her and was careful to keep her arm with the gun pointed down at the ground. She clung to him with her other arm, her body shaking against his. He had almost lost her before he could make things right between them. He could not lose another person he cared for.

"See all the trained men around us? Do you still think you need the gun?" She was handling it well but Tek wasn't comfortable with her being armed in her current emotional state.

Angela looked around and Tek could almost picture her doing the safety math in her head. She nodded and handed the gun back to him which he slipped back into his kidney holster. He wasn't sure he shouldn't have the gun out at this point since the men who had tried to hurt her were still around.

"Boss, the ambulance and cops are at the gate. Should we let them in?" Kane's voice cut off his thoughts.

Tek turned to look at his COO with a raised eyebrow.

Kane sighed. "The man you shot will probably die soon if we delay. Not that I care but probably going to be more paperwork and lawyers if you do that."

There were things that needed to be done and if he was going to keep Angela and Jojo safe he needed to finish as quickly as possible with the police. Things would have been simpler if they hadn't been called, but there were way too many witnesses for that to be a reality. A plan started to form in his mind, and he nodded.

"I want all the lawyers down here immediately and I want the armored car and a five-man protection detail. Once the police are done with us. I'm taking them both to the backup safe house."

"Hawk going to like that plan?" Kane raised an eyebrow.

The backup safe house was in the Dark Sons' compound. His President and Kane knew each other because, in certain circumstances, Hawk occasionally did jobs with Kane's team. The two men had become friends of a sort. The compound was the most secure remote location Tek knew. If he asked, every one of his Brothers would protect his woman. His woman, he snorted. He should probably find out if she was even still talking to him once the stress wore off. He should get Hawk's permission before heading over there. But there was plenty of time for that. He squeezed Angela and knew he wouldn't risk her safety with anyone else.

"I'll call him." Kane nodded and spun away and Tek ran his hand down Angela's hair. "Kitten, the police are coming. I'm going to try and stay by your side but if I can't someone will be nearby to protect you. My lawyers will be here soon, please don't say anything until one of them is with you... Unless you have your own lawyer?"

"I have a lawyer for contracts and taxes, not for something like this."

"Then, for now, use mine."

"We're the victims. Why do we need lawyers?" Her voice was small, but it had lost the mechanical cadence of earlier.

"Until we know what is going on, we need to be careful. Those were well-trained men not some random thugs. Did you piss anyone off lately?"

Angela gave a cute little snort. "Other than you? No, I

haven't done any work in the last two years that would make anyone angry."

Tek saw the lights of both the ambulance and police approaching. Too many things were uncertain right now. The only thing he knew for sure was he wouldn't let anything else bad happen to Angela.

Chapter 22

Hidden agendas piss me off more than butter on a ham sandwich.

T alking with police detectives, even with lawyers at her side, was a new and unpleasant experience. Standing in the parking lot had quickly grown old, but according to the cops, it was go down to the station or remain right where they were. Maybe if she recorded herself saying 'I don't know' it would be easier. Then she could hit a button and every time they came up with a new and unique way of asking her why someone would want to kidnap her.

There were hundreds of reasons someone from her past might want to kidnap her, but nothing recent. Speculating with the police would only accomplish getting herself in trouble. Tek had risked his life to save her and that knowledge ran counter to everything she believed he felt about her. It was easier to believe he didn't care for anyone but himself and his precious company.

Knowing that not only had he come out to check on her,

but risked his safety in the process was throwing her off kilter. His arms wrapped around her was one of the best things in the world. The illusion of safety a welcome fallacy. It had taken all of her acting ability not to break down when the police insisted the witnesses remain separated until their questioning was over. Since she knew nothing, the grilling should've been over a while ago. The lawyer at her side, whose name was Bethany Shortridge, was doing a good job of trying to speed up the police. However, Angela was long past ready to be done with all of this.

"I'm d-done."

The police detective who wasn't very happy with her snapped his gaze to her. "Ms. Turner, you are done when we say you are done."

"Is my client under arrest?" Ms. Shortridge asked.

"We are not finished questioning her." Detective Markin scowled, making his face even less pleasant.

"We've been answering questions for over an hour and you have yet to ask more than the same three questions. If there is nothing new, my client will make herself available at a later date if you come up with something."

Angela tuned out the argument, wanting nothing more than to stamp her feet in frustration. Jojo's questioning had lasted only a few minutes. That may have had more to do with the outrageous way she flirted with the officer questioning her. It was funny to watch how comfortable her friend was with making people uncomfortable. Tek finished his own questioning session almost ten minutes ago, and he had shot someone! Both of them were standing the requested distance away from her questioning, looking almost as frustrated as she was. Why was her interrogation taking so long?

Something was off with the police's behavior. Calculating the odds and variables in her head was easy once she thought to do it. Procedurally they should have offered her protection, but that hadn't happened. They also hadn't been particularly hostile towards her, so she doubted they thought she was responsible. They had been slow and frustratingly exceeded the usual three repetition of questions that police used to make sure a witness had their story straight. All those things only made sense if they were stalling.

"Who are w-we waiting for?" Angela interrupted the argument between her temporary lawyer and the detective.

"Excuse me?"

The detective needed more practice on his poker face because it was obvious to her he was not only surprised but hiding something. There were several possibilities, but the most likely given the time that had passed he was waiting for someone from Denver. If that was true, the person would be here within the next few minutes.

There were so many possibilities, and none of them appealed. Every time she got so much as a parking ticket, some government agent was trying to leverage favor for favor. What would they try to get her to do for witness protection?

"Arrest me or I'm l-leaving." Angela raised her voice so everyone around her heard. "Jojo if you could s-start live-streaming this I'd be appreciative."

Jojo whipped out her phone. "I got you girl we will be trending on Insta in a sec with how hot I look."

Angela walked over to her friend, leaving the sputtering detective to deal with the lawyer or make a scene as Jojo was holding up her phone as if about to start talking to her adoring fans.

Tek's chuckle was a balm against the horrible day. He reached out an arm as if offering her a hug, and it was oh, so tempting. She gave a shake of her head and leaned against the soft leopard skin jumpsuit of her friend instead.

Kane walked up to the three of them, his bulking frame blocking out most of the surrounding scene. He stared at the phone Jojo was holding up till she stopped recording and tucked it away.

"Rick got away during the chaos. I've got men trying to track him down. If you want to get out of here, you better move quickly. I got word the FBI is about fifteen minutes out."

Angela couldn't control the shiver both pieces of news caused. "Where would we go? I really don't know w-why those guys were after me."

Tek's face was tight. "I want to take you both to a safe house until we figure out what is going on."

Jojo put a hand on her hip. "And how exactly do we get past the Popo? They really don't look like they want my girl going anywhere."

"I've got a helicopter around back. Leaving may cause issues down the road, but right now I don't give a shit." Tek must have been as frustrated as she was.

"Ms. Turner." The voice calling her name brought back unpleasant memories of her father's funeral. Even there, this asshole hadn't been decent enough to leave her alone. The man walking up from the parking lot would have been considered handsome to an outsider. Only slightly above average height, he wore his expensive suits well. Brown hair framed sharp features and his friendly smile didn't quite reach his eyes.

Angela forced herself to step away from Jojo and face the man who had been trying to recruit her since she was a teenager. She felt Tek and Kane at her back like an over protective blanket.

"Agent Devin. What agency are you working for this week?"

He chuckled, but it held no warmth. "You know I've been with the DEA for years. Heard you had a bit of trouble and wanted to be sure you were okay."

"With that suit I'm s-surprised. I assumed the NSA, FBI,

or Homeland Security had given you another c-chance." Angela fought to get her nerves under control, but this man was responsible for her forced recruitment as a teenager and brought out the worst in her. He might not have any official power over her anymore, but she knew he still had his fingers in all the pies.

His smile turned into a snarl for a moment. She knew he hated his current assignment and couldn't care less. She had tried to find this man's dirty laundry more than once in hopes of being permanently rid of him, but he was either fantastic at hiding his crimes or was actually an innocent asshole who had a thing for messing with her life.

"No, though I'm here with an offer on behalf of the FBI." His face may have said honest concern, but she had long ago learned he was an expert at lying.

"Of course you are. The answer is n-no."

"You need protection."

Tek stepped forward, placing himself between her and the agent. "The lady said no. She has protection."

"I'm sorry we haven't been introduced. I'm Senior Special Agent Devin. And you are?" Agent Devin's tone was perfectly friendly but Angela could see the anger pinching up the corners of his eyes.

"Joseph Vallier." Tek didn't return the agent's smile.

Surprise flicked across the agent's face. He might not have recognized Tek's face, but understood who he was talking to now. "Don't let her innocent act fool you, Mr. Vallier. She has enemies you wouldn't want to mess with and her loyalty is only to herself."

Jojo snorted. Angela felt a warmth at her friend's unspoken support. This man had tried to isolate her for most of her life, supposedly for the good of the country. He saw her as a criminal, so anything he did was justified.

Tek crossed his arms and seemed to study the agent. "My

company is who the government calls when they are out of their depth, so you'll excuse me if I think she's safer with us."

Angela didn't understand why, once again, Tek was putting himself between her and danger. She wasn't sure she could trust him, but she knew she couldn't trust Agent Devin. She cleared her throat. "As I have said multiple times before, I will never work with or for you."

"You could do so much good if you would just let go of this petty grudge you have. You're in over your head this time."

Tek stepped into Devin's personal space. "Seems to me you know more about this time then we do. Care to share?"

Devin held his ground with a smirk. "Not how this works. You sleeping with her? That doesn't work out so well for her friends or lovers, I'd watch your back." He leaned to the side, catching Angela's gaze. "You know how to contact me when your newest boy toy can't save you. This time you will come to heel."

Kane grabbed Tek from behind as he lunged for the asshole who had threatened her. The agent chuckled for real this time and with a finger salute turned and left.

Angela's body shook with unused adrenaline. After everything the dickhead had done to her over the years, he continued to believe he was the good guy and she the villain. More, he knew things she needed to know, things that could be a danger to her life and instead of trying to help, once again, he was trying to use it to gain control of her.

Tek shrugged off Kane. His anger, unlike Devin's, was almost a beautiful thing. It brought a protective fire to his eyes that made Angela feel safe. She knew she should still be mad at him. A small part of her still was, but a bigger part of her wanted nothing more than to let herself go and for once allow someone else to keep her safe.

"What's your history with that guy?" Tek's voice held an undeniable command.

"Ten years ago he got what was supposed to be the biggest break of his career. All he had to do to get it was terrorize a thirteen-year-old who got caught hacking the military to get his dead father's service record." Angela gave a small laugh. "He convinced my friend, Johnny that not only was he going to go to jail but his mother was going to lose her house and go to jail as well since it was her computer that was used."

"Bastard," Jojo muttered.

"Johnny was like a little brother to me, and I never blamed him for giving up my identity. So Devin had me arrested, although they had no proof of any crimes. While I was being detained, Johnny killed himself out of guilt." The pain of his death was still a sharp pain in her chest.

"They had no proof?" Tek seemed confused.

"Nope. CA-million never takes credit. Rumors, sure. Good guesses, probably. But no proof, not that the government has ever let that stop them. It's not important, but the deal they made included the clause that Agent Devin never worked for the FBI again. I was naïve. They just moved him over to the NSA."

Kane whistled. "No wonder he hates you. You responsible for his other job changes?"

Angela nodded. "He keeps coming after me. Trying to turn friends against me. He moves, I counter. But he hasn't bothered me since my father's funeral. I had hoped he had moved on since the DEA doesn't have any jurisdiction over cyber-crimes."

Tek frowned. "Could he be behind this attack?"

"Unless those guys turn out to be black ops, I don't think so. Devin really believes he is serving his country, and he learned a long time ago that kidnapping me won't get him what he wants."

"Dead Man files?"

Angela shrugged, not wanting to admit too much out in the open.

Kane laughed. "There is a lot more to you than meets the eye."

"My girl has more layers than an onion." Jojo gave her a big hug which was exactly what she needed.

"Mr. Vallier, Ms. Turner." Bethany, her lawyer from earlier, walked up. "The police say you all are free to go and they will contact you if they have any further questions."

Those words relaxed something deep inside Angela. There was so much more to figure out, but it could be done somewhere else. If she was going to be spending time with Tek at a safe house, the two of them needed to figure things out. She would have to decide if giving him a second chance was worth the risk to her heart.

Chapter 23

You can't have fun breaking the rules if there aren't any.

The helicopter ride to the Dark Sons' compound was quiet. Even the flamboyant Jojo remained silent. She had held Angela against her bigger frame the whole time, running a comforting hand down her purple locks. A strange jealousy had filled Tek, not because the drag queen was competition for Angela's body, but because he wanted to be the one comforting her.

It was the first time he had wanted a woman this badly. His possessiveness was a surprise. Listening to the story from her point of view was so different from the picture Max had painted. She was kind and ruthless, innocent and jaded, most of all brilliant and naïve. No single word or idea could hold the complexity that was this woman.

The sight of Hawk waiting for them as they exited the chopper was reassuring. His presence, as always, made him seem larger than life. The President of the MC didn't move as they walked to him, the sound of the helicopter fading into the distance.

"So you decided on stealth? Was a marching band not available?" Hawk's sarcastic tone held only a tinge of annoyance.

Tek clasped arms with his Brother and smiled. "We flew in under the radar and took the long way so we didn't pass over any heavily populated areas. Didn't want to have to shake a tail in a car." He turned to face Angela and Jojo. "Ladies, this is the President of the Dark Sons MC and our current host, Hawk. Hawk, this is Jojo and Angela."

Hawk nodded, a serious expression on his handsome face. "Okay ladies. You're on my compound. Follow the rules and me and my Brothers will keep you safe. You break the rules, and you are out on your asses. Rules are simple if you're not in the house," he nodded to the two-story colonial behind him, "you're with a Brother. You do whatever the Brother says. You don't want to do what he says you return immediately to the house. Easy enough?"

Tek bristled a bit at the thought of Angela going around with another Brother. He needed to get himself in check. Staying with Angela twenty-four seven wasn't practical, no matter what his primal side wanted. The two nodded and Jojo cocked a hip.

"Your Brothers look anything like you, gorgeous, and I will follow them anywhere." Jojo's teasing words made Tek groan, but Hawk only chuckled.

"None of my Brothers swing that way far as I know, but the Old Ladies are going to love you. Try not to cause too much chaos."

"Shame." Jojo sighed. "No promises, but I'll try to behave."

"Good to know. You guys get settled in. Dozer and his Old Lady Val are having a barbeque in an hour if you all want to join. Their house is that one." Hawk pointed across the field to where several of the officers' houses sat.

Tek knew more houses were planned as more Brothers settled down and wanted to live in the compound. Security was top of the line and covered the several-hundred-acre property. The convenience of having his Brothers nearby had been what prompted Tek to build this house here which acted as both a second home for him and a backup safe house when situations were delicate.

Angela's expression of dismay as she looked down at her outfit was adorable. The white blouse was dirty from when she crawled under the car and her knee socks, though still sexy as hell, looked as if they had seen better days. "I don't think I'm dressed for meeting a b-bunch of p-people."

Hawk looked her up and down, then over at the Diva in leopard print which showed several tears from the fight earlier. "Well, you look to be about Val's size so I can get her to send over something. Jojo unless you are okay with jeans, a t-shirt, and combat boots, might be out of luck."

"I can rock any outfit, honey and I will be happy to get out of these heels." Jojo waggled her footwear.

"Thank you, Hawk." Angela smiled.

Tek showed them around the four-bedroom house he had re-fitted with all the modern conveniences. After the tour, Jojo decided to take the first shower, leaving him alone with Angela in the kitchen. He opened the fridge and surveyed the options.

"Water, OJ, or beer?"

"Water, please." She sighed. "I can't believe it's only afternoon. It feels like it should be later."

Tek filled two glasses with water and handed one to Angela. "I know what you mean. So much has happened."

A tiny gurgling growl echoed through the quiet room and Angela's cheeks pinkened. "Guess I'm hungry." She leaned against the counter and winced.

"What's wrong?"

"Just brushed my knee against the island. I think I skinned it when I was under the car."

"Let me look."

Angela shook her head and rolled her eyes. "I will survive some minor scrapes. I'll clean them out when I shower."

"Never said you wouldn't survive. Not the point. Let me see it." That she was hurt in any way and had remained silent bothered him. He needed to see if there was gravel or dirt in the cuts. Why had she spent hours with an injury like that, when he could have had her cleaned up and bandaged hours ago?

She took a drink of her water then did a little kick sideways with one leg sending her skirt flaring. "See." She drew out the e like a child, making him want to chuckle.

He thinned his lips and stared her straight in the eyes. "Young lady front and center." His voice held more of a growl than he had intended, but her smile said she didn't mind it. With an exaggerated march, she stomped over to him and executed a messy salute. He grabbed her by the waist and lifted her up onto the island in one motion. His intent had been to bring the injured area into the light, but he had to bite back a groan at the sexy sight of her in the tiny skirt and white blouse perched up on the marble.

His eyes traveled down her body trying not to linger on the sight of her chest as it moved with her short, startled breaths. The swell of her hips against his hands made him want to clutch onto her, but he resisted. Instead, he ran his hands down the sides of her thighs until he reached the top of her knee socks. Carefully, he pulled the cotton down until he had her kneecaps uncovered.

It wasn't as bad as he feared, the socks had kept any dirt from going into the little cuts he saw on both knees. He ran a light touch over each. "Does this hurt?"

"Not really." Angela's words were breathy. "My guess is only the right one is going to bruise. Will you kiss it and make it better?"

Tek felt his dick come to life as the idea of placing his lips on her filled his mind. He ran his hand up her body to her neck and wrapped his fingers into her hair. With a firm tug, he tilted her head so her beautiful teal eyes locked with his. "You're playing with fire, little girl."

Tek saw her pulse racing against her neck as she swallowed. "I know. I can't seem to stop myself."

"Right now, I want nothing more than to push this little skirt up and see what kind of panties you have on." Tek enjoyed Angela's little groan. "Are you a good girl wearing little white panties confused by how wet she is?" He leaned in and nibbled her ear. "Or a naughty little tease who wears a red thong so I have to punish her for being out of uniform?"

He felt her legs spread wider, as if begging him to follow through. God, how he wanted to, but they had too much still unsettled between them. If he lost himself in this moment, he knew when it was over, things would be worse between them.

Staring into her eyes, he realized he wanted all of this woman, not fleeting moments of play and pleasure, but something lasting. He moved his hand from her hair to cup her face. Unable to resist, he brushed his lips against hers and took a small taste.

Gathering all of his self-control, he stepped back. "We need to talk."

Angela blinked a few times then pulled her legs together, but not before he glimpsed white cotton.

"You're probably right." Her hands fiddled with the edge of her skirt in nervous motions. "I'm not very good at t-talking about h-hard things."

Tek laughed. She hadn't meant her words to be dirty, but it was a perfect example of how innocent she was. He leaned back against the counter across from her and decided it was best to rip off the band-aid.

"Have you forgiven me?"

"I don't know, s-sort of. I trust you with my safety. You put yourself in danger to protect me. You're helping me stay safe, even though you could have handed that duty off to the police. I'm a-attracted to you." The pink flush that filled her cheeks was adorable. "You're smart, and you don't seem to mind m-my quirks."

"Quirks?"

Angela gestured at her outfit. "Roleplaying. I s-started doing it at the club to try to discover who I w-wanted to be. I like who I am, but I love being all those other things too. I love being Cami, and what you did stole the joy of losing myself in a role. Like I h-have to be Angela playing a role rather than being Cami the schoolgirl." She shook her head. "I don't know if I'm making any sense."

Tek nodded. "Trust in any relationship is important. That first time you set the rules, we communicated, but everything after that was fucked up."

The silence in the room that followed his statement was heavy. If he wanted to explore the undeniable chemistry between them, really find out what the two of them might be together, he couldn't accept only part of her. Being a full time dominant for a woman hadn't ever appealed to him because he had thought only of the individual roles that seemed to go along with that dynamic. He liked variety.

The thought of letting Angela slip away, only getting a small taste of paradise was unacceptable. Regaining her trust fully would take work, but he had never backed down from a challenge.

"I think we need rules. Establish expectations so I can regain your trust."

Angela wrinkled her nose. "What, like I have to eat my

vegetables, clean my room, and greet you at the door naked? And you have to say please and give me at least two orgasms a day?"

The bark of laughter that exploded from his chest felt amazing. "Not quite what I was thinking, though I think you are aiming far too low on the orgasm count for the start of negotiations."

She giggled and the musical sound filled the kitchen. "What were you thinking then?"

"The easiest is that we agree not to lie to one another and that no matter what we are doing, the safeword stoplight system will be followed. Even if it is a simple conversation, you can safeword but you can't lie."

"The premise sounds good, but might be a little hard to execute."

"Oh? How is that?"

"Well, I'm not really a schoolgirl, or a secretary, or a slave girl. How do we define lying versus pretending?"

She had a point, but Tek thought he had a solution. "When I call you Angela, I expect nothing but truth. Other times I'll call you little girl, Cami, or slave."

Tek enjoyed the way her eyes dilated and her breathing grew shallow. "So." She swallowed and cleared her voice. "I'll call you something like Master, Daddy, or Mr. Vallier when we are pretending, and Joseph if I want to simply be me?"

Tek was glad he was in suit pants because his dick was so hard it would have been straining uncomfortably against the zipper of his jeans. He was glad she seemed to not only be willing to give him another chance, but eager.

"Yes. Real names are like a safeword. No matter which of us says it, all roleplaying ends. We don't have to stop what we are doing, but we need to be honest and not hide in a role."

Angela bit her lip and nodded. "I think that will work. Why are you doing all of this? I can't imagine it is just because you want to f-fuck me. There have to be hundreds of girls who would be a lot less trouble and a lot more experienced than me."

Tek closed the distance between them and pressed his hard cock against her legs. "Oh, I want you, not going to lie about that. I don't know where this is going or what tomorrow might bring. Call me a caveman if you want, but my honest answer is because I want you to be mine. Mine to protect, mine to pleasure, and mine to explore."

She looked at him with a twinkle of mischief in her eyes. "Caveman isn't a fantasy I've really dreamed about, but I might be convinced."

Tek claimed her mouth and tried to let her feel just how happy she had made him. She met him with a passion that threatened to take his breath away.

"Hope you don't mind, but I found some clothes upstairs that fit." Jojo's voice threw cold water on both of them and they broke apart like teenagers caught necking.

The man who stood in the entrance to the kitchen was so unlike the diva they had traveled with that Tek's thoughts took a moment to adjust.

Joshua was in a pair of relaxed blue jeans and a plain black t-shirt that showed off his muscular arms well. His shaved head and bare face looked so different without the wig and makeup altering his ebony features, it was hard to imagine them as the same person.

"Uhm, I guess you're done with the shower." Angela's blush was slowly working its way up her neck.

Joshua raised a teasing eyebrow. "Been out for a while, sweetie. Guess you were too distracted to notice."

Angela hopped down off the counter and gave both of them a shy smile. "I guess I'll take my shower now."

Joshua gave a chuckle. "Be quick. I'm starving and that barbeque sounds heaven sent."

"Careful, Tek. When Joshua gets hangry, it isn't a pretty sight."

"I'll keep that in mind." Tek watched as Angela scurried out of the kitchen, wanting to follow after her but knowing he needed to give her some space.

Joshua leaned forward and from the serious look on his face, Tek saw he had something on his mind.

"You're not my boss anymore, so I'm going to give it to you straight. If it were up to me, I'd beat the living crap out of you for what you tried to do to that girl. You saved us today and are giving us a safe place, so maybe she thinks the karma scales are balanced. I don't."

Tek clenched his fists. The urge to lash out was there, but this was Angela's best friend and hurting him would crush any hope he had of fixing what he had broken. So he stayed silent.

"She's a grown woman. I heard some of what you two said and I can only hope this isn't some sex game for you. I'll try to keep out of it and be supportive of whatever she chooses, but you should know... I don't care that you're a badass biker billionaire. If you hurt my girl again, I will find a way to make you pay."

Tek respected Joshua for speaking his mind. This man could come between him and Angela if he didn't at least try to make peace. So he gave the man his own truth.

"Getting between us is a bad idea. Not going to say I'm never going to fuck up, but I will never again hurt her on purpose. So out of respect for her, I'm going to forget you threatened me and be glad she has a friend who cares."

"Oh, I care. Break her in any way and you will see just how much I care."

Chapter 24

Who's your Daddy? … No seriously, who?

The relaxed atmosphere and amazing spread of almost gourmet food was not what Angela had imagined when she imagined a biker barbeque. The weathered picnic table she sat at was well maintained. Her stomach ached from the amazing food she had eaten. Joshua was laughing near the grills, chatting with a group of women. The way he could make friends at a moment's notice made her a tad jealous.

She felt like a social idiot sitting away from everyone trying not to freak out because she was surrounded by strangers. At least Tek had taken pity on her and kept her company while she ate enough for five large men. Now that she had adjusted to her surroundings, she was embarrassed by her own assumptions. This wasn't a wild drunken event that she should fear.

If anything, it was more like a neighborhood get-together. Well, if all the men were ex-military hotties who wore black leather vests with patches on them and the neighborhood was in an enclosed compound.

The biker outlaw culture had been briefly covered in one of her sociology classes as an example of closed societies that exist within the modern world. What she was seeing didn't fit within anything she had learned. There were more men than women, but those present looked happy, not like oppressed slaves only used for sex or service. A few of the ladies were dressed like rocker chicks, but others would fit in at any PTA meeting. She had on jeans and a sparkly t-shirt that said, *'Ride or Die'*.

The men had less variety in style. Even Tek had changed into what seemed to be the uniform of tight, well-worn jeans, a t-shirt, and vest. Some of the patches on the men's vests matched, but most had lots of extras that were all different.

Angela studied the worn black leather on Tek's back. "What do the patches on your vest mean?"

"It's a cut, not a vest." Tek chuckled.

Angela rolled her eyes. "Okay. What do the patches on your cut mean?"

"Sorry. Think of it like the military. Everyone has their club and chapter on the back, it's like a branch of service." He gestured to his chest. "Name and rank. The rest are accomplishments or sometimes events we've been to."

She nodded to his shoulder. "The 1% means you don't follow the law."

"It's more complicated than that. Being a 1%er means different things to different clubs. To the Dark Sons it means that laws aren't as important as the club. That we would do anything regardless of consequence for the good of our Brothers and their families."

"Do your Brothers go to jail a lot?"

"Sometimes, but not as much as you would think. Unlike

some clubs, we keep ourselves tight and only break the law when it is worth the risk."

Angela remembered her own less than legal activities. Didn't she do exactly the same thing when she chose her sense of right over what was legal? "I guess I can understand that."

"I thought you might. Would you like some dessert? Pixie makes some of the best cookies on the planet."

Angela looked down and saw she had eaten every bite on her plate. "If they are half as good as the food, absolutely."

"You going to come with?"

Angela was enjoying the people watching and wasn't ready to dive into meeting his Brothers yet. "Do you mind if I stay here? I promise I'll put on my social hat in a few."

He stood and kissed her on the head. The sight of him as he walked away was a treat. His ass could win any contest it wanted to. Angela giggled at her own silliness. Every man here probably did hundreds of squats a day. She hadn't enjoyed working out herself until she found the pole dancing class. She had even installed a pole in her spare bedroom so she didn't have to face the boredom of free weights ever again.

"Hi. I'm Pixie, you must be Angela."

Angela spun around, startled. She hadn't heard anyone approaching. The tiny blonde woman standing directly behind her wasn't a threat, but her heart pounded for a few more moments while her brain caught up.

The woman was dressed in an adorable dress that showed off her obvious baby bump. Green eyes that seemed friendly studied her as she caught her breath.

"Sorry, didn't mean to startle you. Do you mind if I sit?"

"N-no, go ahead."

Her face was so familiar. Angela pummeled her mind for where she recognized the woman from. Had she come into the strip club? No, a pregnant woman there would have stood out.

She smiled, and it was like the sun coming out from behind a cloud. The pieces fell into place and Angela's body froze.

It was the girl from her files. The smile of the small child perfectly mirrored in an adult face. Tek's sister. And she had sat down next to her on the picnic bench. Did he know his sister was here? He had to, right?

The woman sat and nodded towards where Tek had gone. "That's my old man, Sharp, talking to Tek."

Tek was smiling, talking to a man with brown hair and a scruffy jawline. Angela couldn't focus on them since her own brain was going in circles. She stared at the woman, reviewing the file she had briefly read. Remembering all the photos she had spent hours creating as she aged the little girl into an almost exact replica of this adult woman.

"Oh my God. I'm staring, that is so rude of me. I didn't expect to see you here. It's so nice to meet you, Phoebe, or do you go by Nicole now? Wait, you said Pixie. So, I guess you picked a new name." Angela was babbling but couldn't seem to stop. That Tek had found his sister after all this time must have been so exciting and now, he was going to be an uncle.

Pixie pulled back a look of suspicion on her face. "How do you know my name? Did Tek tell you about me?"

"No. I mean his sister being kidnapped at age four is public knowledge and I wanted to help so I used aging software and some searches. I got the results with your information this morning. Then someone tried to kidnap me, so I got distracted, but I guess he found you on his own. So, I don't need to tell him."

Pixie had gone pale and Angela got concerned.

"I'm s-sorry if I'm babbling. I'm just glad he found you. It's like a fairy tale. Kid from foster care finds out they are actually a billionaire heiress kidnapped from their family."

"Sharp!" Pixie's strangled cry was loud.

Angela shot up. "I'll get him. Is it the baby?" She spun to

run towards the food table and bounced off a chest of solid muscle. She staggered back a few steps and realized Sharp must have heard her because he was now kneeling in front of his woman.

Tek wrapped an arm around her side, steadying her.

"What's wrong, darlin'?" Sharp ran a gentle hand down Pixie's arm.

Pixie pointed at Angela. "She said… She said…" was all she seemed to be able to get out.

Angela tried to figure out what she had said that had so upset the woman. Sure, she had been babbling, but—

"What the fuck did you say to my woman?" Sharp was in her face, his anger, a physical force that knocked all thoughts out of her brain.

Tek pulled her behind him. "Calm down, Brother."

Joshua seemed to appear out of nowhere and placed himself at Tek's shoulder. With the wall of friendly men between her and the very scary man, her thoughts kicked into gear and she gasped.

Angela leaned to the side and caught Pixie's eyes. "Y-you didn't know?"

Pixie shook her head. Angela paced, embarrassed to have dropped a bomb on the woman.

"I'm so sorry. I didn't know. I mean, I assumed, you're here, he's here, how could you not know?"

Tek grabbed her shoulders to hold her still. "What didn't she know?"

Angela's thoughts swirled trying to figure out how to make up for dropping something so important on a pregnant woman. "That she's your sister."

Tek stumbled back as if punched, and Angela felt awful. She had done it again!

Joshua held her steady, looking around at the scene that was forming. More Brothers had come over and the women were gathering around Pixie as if trying to block her from danger.

It made no sense, shouldn't everyone be happy? Joshua tipped her chin up. "Sweetie, you need to back up to the beginning so we can all catch up to where your brilliant mind has jumped."

Angela looked at Tek and realized he looked as shell-shocked as Pixie.

"The beginning. Okay." She wiped her sweaty hands on the sides of her shirt. "So, after I met you the second time I thought if I did something nice for you, maybe you might want to get to know me better and overlook my uhm..." Angela looked around and realized there would be no saving herself embarrassment. "Lack of experience."

Tek nodded, his confusion seeming to grow. She powered on. "I'd heard about your sister's kidnapping seventeen years ago. Well, seventeen years ago facial recognition software sucked, and most records weren't searchable. Aging software has come really far since then as well, so I figured I might be able to get you closure even if it was only proof she had died."

Comprehension started forming on Tek's face. She looked at Joshua. "Remember when I said we had to go back inside?" Joshua nodded. "The data mining program I'd started had found something. Look."

Angela pulled out her phone and pulled up the photos. "Nicole Vallier, age four." The photo she showed them all was of a smiling blonde child with bright green eyes in expensive clothes, her hair done up in ringlets. She swiped the screen to the next photo. "Jane Doe renamed Phoebe Smith six months later." The girl in the photo was skinnier, with dirty hair and bruised green eyes. As she flipped back and forth, the resemblance was apparent.

"The aging program I did on the original photo matches

the photos in Phoebe's Foster records. Here is the one of her at her current age."

The computer-generated photo was almost an exact match for the stunned woman sitting at the picnic table.

"When I saw her here, I guess, I assumed you knew."

Tek shook his head, then looked over at Pixie with a look of wonder that filled Angela's heart.

"I think Pixie and Tek could use a moment. Everyone give them some space." Hawk's voice cut through the stunned silence like a blade.

Angela backed away with Joshua at her side, not sure where to go. A table a little ways away looked like it held desserts. She decided a sugar fix was the perfect solution to her stress.

She looked back, making sure Tek was all right.

Joshua snorted. "You have it bad for that man, don't you?"

"Yeah. I think I do."

"After what he did, you're still going to give him your treasure."

Angela giggled. "My treasure?"

Joshua waved a hand. "Your V-card, your honeypot, your budding flower. What I call it is not the point. You are going to lie down with a man who hurt you so bad you came sobbing to my door at one a.m. and spent the night proving what an ass he was."

"I can't explain it but, yeah, I think I am."

Joshua studied her like she might have the secrets of the universe etched somewhere on her face. "Okay. You are a big girl so you make your own choices but know I will always be there for you."

Joshua wrapped her up in a big hug, then let her go.

"Besides, I don't know if he'll even want me anymore after I botched telling him about his sister."

"Honey, that was like a Fairy tale meets Jerry Springer." Joshua's flippant comment seemed to break the serious mood.

"No kidding. That had to be the worst way I could have broken the news. I thought she was going to pass out."

"Nah. Our Pixie is like a willow branch, she bends but she don't break." Angela turned towards the voice dripping with a southern accent. The owner of the voice was a woman who was the spitting image of a red-headed young Dolly Parton. Her jeans were painted on and her sparkly top hugged cleavage that was almost too big to be real. She stuck out her hand. "I'm Val."

"I'm Cami, I mean Angela." Angela sighed. Her southern accent, much like Joshua's when in his Jojo persona, had made her slip for a moment.

"No worries, honey bunch. My proper name's Sue-Ann, so you just tell me what you prefer to be called and we'll go with that."

What did she prefer? Cami and CA-million were alter-egos that she fell back on when she was doing something wild or outside the bounds of the very strict rules she had placed on her life. Did she want to be Angela the boring stuttering introvert or Cami the risk taker who danced on stage and lived life by her own rules?

"I think I want to be Cami."

"You go for it, girl." Joshua patted her on the shoulder then held out a hand to Val. "I'm Joshua but when I look half as fabulous as you, people call me Jojo. I just have to know where you got those boots and if they come in my size."

Cami looked down and saw that Val was wearing a pair of black, knee-high, wedge boots with rows of rhinestones down the side. She held her breath, wondering how the woman would react to her flamboyant friend. Val cocked her hip, looking Joshua up and down.

"Think you can walk in these?"

"Oh, I can walk, dance and as my girl will attest, kick ass in those heels," Joshua snapped as if demanding she talk.

"No doubt. Jojo took out two of my attackers today wearing six-inch heels."

"Like that, is it?" Val smiled. "Teach me to judge a flower by its bud. Well, I'll happily take you to the boutique in Denver where I find most of my fabulous footwear. Can't say they will have your size, but I'm sure they can special order what they don't have."

"Fabulous." Joshua gave a surprised Val an enthusiastic hug.

"So you're Tek's woman?"

"Well, he brought me here, if that's what you mean. We're something, but I wouldn't say I'm his." Cami wasn't sure what they were yet. Heading towards something, but not there yet.

Joshua snorted. "If you're not his, what was all that caveman 'mine' shit I walked in on in the kitchen?"

Cami giggled. "Oh God. Tell me you didn't hear that!"

"Every testosterone laced word from the safewords on."

"Why didn't you say something?"

"Safewords? Huh, and here I thought Tek was the most vanilla of the Brothers."

"Oh my God! Stop it both of you."

The two laughed and gave each other a high five. Guess her best friend had found a partner in crime. The idea of Jojo teaming up with Val had hilarious disaster written all over it.

Val gave her a wink. "You come over to the Clubhouse on a Friday or Saturday night and you will see a whole new side of the Brothers. We may like our family time, but we love our grownup time even more. But seriously, these men don't bring casual to family events like this, so I'm guessing it won't be long before you're wearing his cut."

"Doesn't the cut mean you're a Dark Son?" Cami was confused by all the new information she was having to take in.

Val twisted so her back showed. On the top was the same Dark Sons logo the men wore, but the bottom of the patch didn't read Denver, instead it said, *'Property of Dozer'*. "All of the women here are Old Ladies, but we usually only wear our cuts when going out or if civilians are present. Ever since Dozer found out I was pregnant, he has insisted on it. Says it makes him feel secure that people know who I belong to."

There was no sign of a baby bump on Val, so she assumed it was recent news. "Congratulations! Guess there is something in the water."

"You pregnant too?" Val seemed excited by the thought.

"Not unless there is a holy star rising in the north," Joshua snarked.

"Hey! Not nice." He was right, but still.

Val's jaw dropped as she obviously got the Jesus reference. "Let me get this straight. You're a virgin, who is with Tek, and talking about safewords. How kinky are you?"

Joshua burst out laughing. "Even crazier, her side hustle is as a stripper at Darklights. That is how they met."

"Lord, give me strength. I thought I had heard it all." Val looked her up and down with an assessing eye. "You any good?"

"At stripping?"

"Yeah. I always wanted to learn those tricks the girls do on the pole to drive Dozer wild."

"I think I could teach you a trick or two." Cami smiled.

The three of them burst into laughter. Her life was pretty crazy. She looked over to where Tek sat with his sister. The two of them sat gripping each other's hands. Their expressions of happiness clear even at this distance. He was a good man who had done some bad things. But hadn't they all? Maybe it was time to give in to her desires. What fantasy worked best to convince a man to make her first time unforgettable?

Chapter 25

The truth will set you free, or fuck you up. Your choice.

T ek stared at Pixie with fresh eyes. He could see bits of both their parents in her features now that he knew what to look for. They both had blond hair and while he had his father's pale blue-gray eyes, she'd inherited their mother's green ones.

Months they had known each other and not once did he notice what was right in front of him. Even her laugh, though deepened with age, held the musical quality he remembered from the little girl he'd chased around the yard.

"Is she right? Am I your sister?" Pixie's voice trembled.

"I don't think she'd make it up. From what I've heard, she's the best at what she does." Tek ran a nervous hand through his hair. "I'm so sorry I didn't find you sooner. It must be hard to believe, but I never gave up looking. Though apparently, I'm shit at picking PIs. All these years and millions of dollars and they brought me nothing. She finds you in one day."

Tek would take the hide out of someone. If he'd only found her sooner, his sister would never have gone through the hell of the last year. Abducted, raped, and fleeing a psychotic mobster, it was only luck his Brother Sharp had been there to rescue her.

"No." Pixie grabbed his hand and squeezed. "You can't go down that path. We can't think like that. Nothing can change the past and I'm happy where I am." She placed a hand on her stomach and looked over at Sharp, who was sitting a few tables over with concern written across his face.

"You love him?" Those two had something special, but the question needed to be asked.

"Yes, more than anything."

"You sure? 'Cause Angela wasn't wrong, you are now a very wealthy woman. Our parents kept your trust fund, and we all put into it every year. I continued putting in even after their deaths. I think it was the only thing we three ever agreed on. Keeping hope alive."

"Our parents are dead?" Pixie looked down at her hands.

"Mom died of cancer five years ago. Dad in a car accident a year later." Their father had been drunk and angry all the time, mourning his wife and daughter. No one believed the crash was an accident. But she didn't need to know that.

"Oh." Her crestfallen expression tore at his heart.

"They loved you dearly. I'm sorry you won't ever get to meet them."

"It's weird that an hour ago I was happy. In my mind, my family was long dead. Now my whole world tipped sideways, and I am upset I'll never get to meet parents I didn't know I had. Add in the money thing and none of this feels real."

Tek gave her a small teasing smile. "Well, it is real enough that you never have to settle if you don't want to. You can ditch all these peasants and go live the life of a queen."

She laughed, and Tek was glad to see the sadness lift from her eyes. She lifted her nose and put on an adorable snooty accent. "I don't know, I have awfully expensive tastes. It would take a lot to keep me in the lifestyle I've become accustomed to."

Tek chuckled. "Well, last I checked, you have over five hundred and forty million in trust."

Pixie choked and started coughing. Sharp sprinted to her side seconds after she made the first sound of distress.

"You okay?" Sharp rubbed her back.

"Yeah, Sharp, I'm fine. Tek surprised me that's all." She gave Tek wide eyes. "That number isn't a joke?"

"Nope. I was letting my sister know she doesn't have to be a kept woman anymore."

Sharp shot him a glare. "So you're sure she's your sister?" Sharp asked.

"Yeah. It will take a DNA test to unlock the funds, but I'm convinced."

"So I might be your sister, and a millionaire?"

Tek nodded, not sure he could talk around the lump in his throat.

Pixie leaned forward and gave him a hug. "We should take this one step at a time. Today has been overwhelming."

"We've got a lifetime to catch up. You should probably go rest." Tek wanted to process everything himself. His week had been filled with so much change, and from the multiple calls he had ignored in the last half hour alone, it didn't look like it was slowing down any time soon.

Hawk walked over, his face serious. "Kane called me since he couldn't get you. I can tell him to pound sand if you want, but it sounded serious."

Sharp stood, helping Pixie to her feet. "I was about to take

Pixie back to our place, anyway. Text me if you need anything, Brother."

They exchanged backslapping hugs. Tek felt a strange peace as he watched the two walk away. It was like a weight that had been riding his shoulders had slipped to the ground. His sister was alive and being watched over by a man he would trust with his life and already part of the family he had chosen for himself.

His phone vibrated in his pocket again, and he answered. "Yeah."

"Christ, you're a hard man to get a hold of." Kane's voice held none of its usual teasing tone.

"Well, you have me now." He shouldn't take out his frustration on Kane, but Tek found he had no patience for the usual back and forth.

"All right then. Lisen instituted the fix your girl suggested herself and says the customers' servers are back online. Need your authorization to run the CIA level background checks she is demanding on every programmer we have. She's driving me crazy and saying no one works on any live code till they pass it."

Tek pinched his nose in frustration. "Start the checks but tell Lisen she is going to have to keep everyone working until you are finished or there won't be a company anymore. If she has specific people, she is concerned about, move them to the top of the list."

"Is there any way you can sweet talk Angela into helping us out? The amount of data she pulled in only a few hours is impressive."

"You do realize all that data was obtained illegally, right?"

"Figured. We need to find Rick. Those names and emails she pulled are for some heavy hitters. Outside the usual scumbag corporations, he tried to sell shit to Russians, Mexicans, and even a few guys from the middle east. FBI is freezing us out in the investigation into the attack earlier, but we got facial recognition on two of them and it's not good."

"What do you have?"

"Mercenaries out of South Africa, high dollar." Kane's sigh was clear even through the phone. "Don't think your girl read through all the data she sent us or she would've known she was in danger."

"What do you mean?" Tek wanted to reach through the phone and drag the information out of his friend.

"Rick sent an email from his not-so-secret account on Thursday saying he had a problem with a nosy coworker to an account linked to a Russian hacking group. They are big time into identity theft but have been known to do other jobs for hire."

"Did he give specifics on her?"

"Name and a photo. They set up to have her followed and taken from home."

"Why did they come into the facility then?"

"Don't know, but we do know before we could pick him up, he called a burner phone from his cell and the call lasted just over a minute."

"Fuck! How did he get away?"

"All you said was to bring him to your office and make sure he didn't leave. When the man down alert went out, forgive me if I thought that was more important than a desk jockey about to get yelled at."

Kane was probably beating himself up now that he knew the whole story. Pulling on that guilt wouldn't help anyone. It was as much his fault for not explaining more at the time.

"It's been a long fucking week. I shouldn't have yelled. How did he get off the property?"

"Walked out to his car and left. You know there is no security on the way out. We've got men on his apartment, but he ditched his phone so we can't track him that way."

"You think they'll keep coming after her?"

"Group like that gets their hands on a hacker like her, they'd be set for life. Depends on how much they're willing to spend on the possibility she'd work under duress."

"So in other words, we have no idea. Okay. Anything else?"

Kane hesitated. "What happened between you and Lisen? She's always a ball-buster, but I'm starting to get the impression she actually hates you."

"Long story. Not the right time. She and I will work something out."

At least he hoped they would. Maybe he should turn over the digital side of the house to her and focus back on what he originally wanted the company to do.

"All right. Don't ghost me again this is not the time to go silent. I'll reach out if anyone picks up anything else on Rick or your girl."

"Right." Tek hung up the phone and realized Hawk was still standing there.

Tek looked over and saw Angela laughing with Joshua and Val. He wanted more than anything to go over, wrap her in his arms and keep her safe from the world. Night darkened the sky and most of his Brothers had headed over to the Clubhouse or back home with their families.

His company had been betrayed, and its information sold to criminals. He'd found a woman so interesting she made him imagine the future. Then he had betrayed that same woman, she had almost been taken from him, and somehow she was still willing to give him a chance. His sister was alive and well. And the woman who made that all possible might still be in danger.

It was enough to drive any man insane. And the week wasn't over.

Hawk crossed his arms. "What do we need to know?"

Tek ran a hand through his hair, trying to pare it all down. "Angela's either in the clear or neck deep in shit. With the week I'm having, I'm guessing in the clear is unlikely."

"What kind of enemy are we talking about?"

"Most likely, the Russians."

"Bratva?" Hawk seemed surprised.

The club had some ties within the Russian mafia that might help if it was them. "Unfortunately, I don't think so. Kane would have mentioned a connection. A hacking group is behind things as far as we can tell. Most of those were created by ex-KGB and only work loosely with the families."

"Get me their name. I have some contacts I might be able to work."

Tek nodded, not surprised. Many of the Brothers had come out of the blacker side of the military. Tek hadn't. He had trained those men to survive. Seen the aftereffects of having to use those skills. Men who had broken, and those who hadn't. Either way, you came out changed.

The people who wanted Angela were as bad as those he faced in war. He wouldn't let them get their hands on her.

Chapter 26

Don't be afraid to ask because you just might get what you are longing for.

The quick connection she had established with these people today was an anomaly. Val reminded her of Jojo so much she had asked if they were spirit sisters separated at birth. Then she had met Tari and her Old Man Dragon. The weird practice these bikers had of calling each other Old made her want to giggle because they were anything but old.

Tari reminded her of the Egyptian queens from old style movies while Dragon was her silent warrior. Their daughter Citlali was a giggling burst of joy, combining the best of her parents' features into a toddler version of absolute adorable beauty.

Guilt for putting all these wonderful people in danger gnawed at her and she offered to leave. Tari had been a warm, calming presence who put her at ease. She told her own story of danger and how the Dark Sons had saved her. Then Val had recounted a bit of Pixie's crazy tale, assuring that not only were the Dark Sons willing to help, they were more than capable.

Dozer had joined them as the sun crept towards the horizon, his love for Val etched in his every feature. The idea of belonging to something so much bigger than herself was appealing for more than the safety it represented. These people were a family by choice, if not by blood.

She jumped as hands gripped her shoulders and caused the group to chuckle. Cami looked up to see Tek smiling behind her.

"Didn't mean to startle you, kitten."

Cami blushed at her overreaction to his touch. "Why do you call me kitten?"

Tek shrugged. "It fits. You're playful, curious, and likely to stumble into a mess."

Joshua clapped his hands. "He's got you there, Cami."

Tari laughed, leaning against Dragon. "Now you are going to have to choose which name you like better."

Cami shook her head and gestured at her hair. "I th-think chameleon is more appropriate."

Her joke had everyone chuckling. Tek leaned down to talk against her ear. "You're going by Cami now?"

"It fits who I want to be," she whispered back.

"Okay, but our deal still stands, little girl." He gave a sweet kiss to her cheek.

Cami's nipples tightened at the memory of their earlier conversation. Heat pooled low in her body as she prayed it meant they were going to do more than talk later. Would he be willing to play the firm but kind Master with his Virgin slave?

Val's voice cut through her dirty daydreams. "Tek, I was telling Joshua he might be more comfortable staying in Dragon's old apartment near the Clubhouse."

"And I," Cami said, "was saying we aren't sure it was me

those guys were after. Better not to have to protect two buildings."

Tek squeezed her shoulders. "Actually, we do. It was in the emails you gave us. Rick arranged for you to be eliminated."

"That weaselly son of a hooker." Joshua's voice expressed Cami's indignation.

"But how did he know I had figured out what he was doing?"

"You must have said something. Why did he send you home early yesterday?"

Cami groaned. "I said his code was crap and full of security loopholes."

"So he wanted you taken out before you figured out the same code was already in the field." Tek's voice rumbled against her and she leaned back with a groan.

"So I can go home and sleep on my thousand count cotton sheets?" The hope in Joshua's voice made her guilt flare. She was the reason he had been dragged into this mess. "If you need me, girl, you know I'm here, but I think you have all the bodies you need to guard you."

She would have agreed to let him go, but Tek spoke instead. "Rick knows you're connected. Until we find him and track down the people hunting her, you could be used to lure her out. We won't force you to stay…"

"But I'd be a fool to go. And my momma didn't raise no fool. I will however take Dragon up on his nice offer. I love you to bits, girl, but I do not need to hear you two getting to know each other better."

"I don't have a problem with that," Tek agreed.

Val gave her a cheeky wink. "On that note, I think we all have places to go or people to do."

Val swept everyone away in a flurry of southern enthusiasm. As each person said their goodbyes, the excitement of what tonight might bring bubbled in her stomach. Would she need to seduce him? Should she be aggressive or shy?

When he took charge, it was like everything in her mind calmed and she was able to enjoy what was happening. He seemed to enjoy being in control, but would he like her to be the aggressor? The men at the club had enjoyed when she put on the dominatrix show. Cami wrinkled her nose.

"What are you thinking about, kitten?" Tek's voice had a slight chuckle.

"That I don't enjoy being a dominatrix." Cami looked around at the now empty field they were standing in.

There were four houses that backed up to the area they had held the barbeque in. The house they were staying in was further away. There was probably enough room they could build another ten houses along the edge of the field without anyone being too close.

Tek chuckled. "I guess it's good I don't like being dominated then, isn't it?" He stepped closer and brushed a lock of hair away from her face. "What triggered that thought?"

The heat radiating from his body in the early evening was welcome. It wasn't winter yet, but autumn nights could be chilly in Colorado. She had promised not to lie to him, but explaining the dizzying amount of thoughts running through her mind was complicated.

"Everyone left us alone because we are supposed to have sex, but since I've never had sex, I'm not sure what to do. So I thought maybe I'm supposed to seduce you. Which made me think of my acts at the club. And while I learned how to crack a whip, I wouldn't enjoy actually whipping someone."

Tek grabbed her chin and kissed her, cutting off the babble she couldn't seem to stop. His mouth was like a gentle claiming. She couldn't resist responding to the sparks that shot through her body. When he finally let her go, her heart was racing, but her mind had calmed.

Tek brushed a thumb over her lips. "Most women would want candlelight, flowers, and sweet seduction for their first time. You, my unique genius, are wondering if there will be whips involved." He ran his hand down her throat with a gentle stroke.

"Is it weird that candlelight and flowers sound excruciatingly boring?"

The light caress of his fingers as they trailed down her chest sent chills down her arms. "No, not weird at all. I'm not going to lie to you, Cami, if this wasn't your first time, I'd take you to the ground right here and make you scream so loud we'd have everyone in the houses coming out to check on you." Pleasure shot through her body when he flicked one of her nipples.

The idea of fucking him in such a primal way appealed to her. She shook her head. "Not the first time, but maybe later?"

"I think we can do that. Should we go back to the house and see where things go?" He ran a gentle hand down her back and cupped her ass.

"No!" Cami regretted her shouted protest when Tek stepped back with his hands to his sides. His look of confusion was clear even in the dim lights from the nearby house.

He looked so handsome in his tight t-shirt and leather vest, and she was already screwing this up. Cami growled in frustration.

"If we see where things go, I'll think. If I think, I'll analyze. I don't want to think. I don't want to choose." How could she make him understand? "You know what, never mind. I'll just die a virgin." She spun and started walking towards the house they were staying at. Being dramatic wasn't usually her style, but the stress of today was overwhelming.

"Angela, stop and look at me."

The command in his voice forced her body to obey before

she processed the words. "What?" The frustration in her voice was embarrassing.

His gray eyes held hers with an intensity and hunger that sent a shiver down her spine. "I need you to be crystal clear about what you are asking for. I'm not a mind reader. Tell me exactly how you want tonight to go."

Embarrassment couldn't actually kill someone, right? It was so much easier to pretend it didn't matter. She could probably fake normal if she had to, but she had waited so long and he was the first man she had met who might not only be willing, but want to fulfill her fantasies.

No guts, no glory. She straightened her shoulders and spoke. "I want to be a slave you purchased for pleasure. I want to have no choices or decisions, but I don't want you to take me until I beg for it. I want to be so out of control that I would do anything to have your cock deep inside me." Tek's glare had become almost feral. "Can we do that?"

"What are your safewords, slave?"

Anticipation had her nipples painfully hard. "Joseph. Yellow. Red."

"You need them, you use them because they're the only things that are going to stop me tonight. Do you understand?"

"Yes, Master."

Before she could internally celebrate, Tek had rushed and lifted her up and over his shoulder. Stunned, she took a moment to catch her breath as she hung upside-down watching the ground pass quickly as he strode across the field with ground devouring strides.

"What are you doing?" Cami struggled to get down. Tek was in impressive shape, but she was a curvy girl. Slinging her around might hurt his back then all their plans for the evening would be ruined.

A sharp sting across her ass interrupted her thoughts. "Slaves don't speak without permission. Keep it up and the first thing I'll do to you when we get inside is turn this ass crimson."

Cami stilled, not sure if the idea of him spanking her scared or excited her. This was so much better than she had imagined. The evidence of her excitement was soaking her panties.

"Good girl."

His firm grip and commanding voice helped her sink into the fantasy. Faster than she imagined they were entering the house, the warm air a welcome change from the cooling night.

Her hair blocked her view as they walked through at least two rooms. She was startled when she was tossed onto a soft surface. She scrambled to look around and didn't recognize the lavish bedroom.

She was on a king-sized bed in the middle of an enormous bedroom decorated in gray and black. Tek had his back to her and was removing a gun she hadn't known he had from the small of his back, placing it on top of an ebony dresser. He took off his watch, then his cut, placing them beside the gun.

He turned and crossed his well-defined arms and gave her a look filled with heat.

"Strip." His command was almost a growl.

"What?" Cami was trying to focus, but the sight of his perfect body in the fitted jeans and tight t-shirt had her distracted.

"I want to see what I've bought. Take those clothes off and let me inspect you."

Cami's hands trembled as she lifted her borrowed shirt over her head. She slid off the side of the bed. She swayed her hips as she pushed her hair over her shoulder, revealing the purple bra she wore. Slowly she worked her pants down her legs, staying bent over with her ass on display as she pulled off her socks and shoes. She eased up slowly, creeping her hands behind her back, undoing her bra. The air hit her nipples as the fabric fell away and a jolt of arousal tightened her core. His growl as she slipped down her panties was exciting. Naked, she bit her lip to try to hide her smile and looked down like a good slave girl.

"Hands behind your back. Chin up."

The position had her exposed. Tek stalked forward, his eyes studying every inch of her exposed skin. He circled her slowly, and she swore she could actually feel his gaze. When he was behind her, he stopped and her legs trembled as she wondered what he was doing.

"Kneel."

Her legs buckled at the command and he caught her with strong hands and helped her to the ground. He moved in front of her, so close all she could see was the front of his jeans with his impressive erection. His finger ran slowly down her cheek and circled her lips. He pressed his finger into her mouth, pressing down on her tongue.

"Have you ever tasted a man, slave?"

"No." Her answer was muffled by the finger that made her vulnerable in a strange new way.

He gripped her by the hair and forced her to look up the length of his body. "What do you call me?"

"Sorry, Master. No, I've never tasted a man." Her core tightened, loving the slight pain of being manhandled. The truth was, her only experience with a man other than Tek had been some awkward petting.

Tek pulled her up to her feet, then to her tiptoes by her hair, and she couldn't hold back the moan of pleasure. His other hand started first flicking, than pinching her nipples. The pressure was gentle at first but then became stronger, sending jolts of pleasure straight to her pussy.

Her mouth grew dry as she panted. Helpless to do anything but take the pleasure, her muscles trembled. She reached out, needing something to grab onto, unable to control the way he was making her body writhe. A sharp slap to one breast than the other shocked her. Pain blossomed across her chest then faded into a wave of warmth.

"Hands behind your back, slave."

"Yes, Master." Cami struggled with the command, finally gripping her wrists behind her to keep from reaching out.

"Good girl." He let her sink back to flat feet, slowly letting go of her hair. He circled behind her, pressing his hard body against hers and trapped her hands between them. He reached around and pulled her close in a hug that was more of a restraining hold.

She was completely helpless, even her air was restricted by his tight hold.

"Do you know what I'm going to do to you?" His breath was hot against her shoulder.

"No, Master."

"I'm going to turn you into my little slut. By the time I'm done with you, you're going to beg me to take your innocence. Beg for even the smallest taste of my cock."

She shook her head, knowing it was true but wanting to fight a little longer. His hold released suddenly, and she took in a gasped breath that made her lightheaded. His hand closed around her throat in a firm grip. She thrashed, scared, and wanted to claw at his hand, but her arms were still trapped between their bodies. His grip loosened slightly, and her panic lessened.

"Give me your color, slave."

It took Cami a minute to understand the question. Her body muscles loosened, and she leaned into his grip. "Green, Master."

He bit her earlobe and whispered against her neck. "Good." Tek's other hand slid down her stomach and cupped her bare pussy. "So wet for me already. I think you already want me inside you."

She shook her head, though her mind and pussy both screamed in protest. The evidence of her lie was leaking down the inside of her thigh, but she didn't want the game to end so soon.

His fingers slid between the lips of her pussy and grazed her clit, sending a surprise orgasm shuddering through her body. A hard wet slap against her clit cut the pleasure short, and she whimpered.

"You're a greedy little slave, aren't you?" He gave a slap to each of her breasts.

It shouldn't feel good, but it did, and she arched her back, wanting more.

"You aren't supposed to come without permission."

"Sorry, Master. I didn't mean to."

He gave each of her nipples a harsh twist that was painful, but then morphed into pleasure so sweet she almost came again. His playing with her nipples earlier had somehow turned everything into a sensual delight.

He stepped back, letting go of her completely. She swayed for a moment, bereft at the loss of his touch.

"Lie down on the bed and grab the headboard."

Cami followed his instructions, her body humming with need. He strode across the room and disappeared into a closet she hadn't noticed. He came out with what looked like silk ties in his hand.

He used them to secure her wrists to the metal headboard. The image of him leaning over her fully clothed while she was bound naked was something she knew she would always fantasize about.

He reached back and pulled off his shirt in a swift motion that had her whimpering at the sight of his well-defined chest. In moments he was completely naked, and Cami didn't think she had ever seen even pictures of a man more gorgeous than him.

"Now I have to punish you for coming without permission."

"Punish?" The word was more of a squeak as it came out of Cami's mouth.

He sat on the edge of the bed and began slowly twisting one of her nipples till the pleasure ebbed into pain. "What do you call me?"

"Master!"

He let go and his mouth replaced his fingers. The intense sensation had her squirming in seconds, moaning and arching up into him.

He sat up. "Normally I would edge you for hours for breaking that rule, but tonight I'm feeling generous."

"Thank you, Master." Cami remembered the short edging he had done while they were in the club and wasn't sure she could survive hours of that.

"Don't thank me yet, slave." He opened the nightstand drawer and pulled out several things Cami couldn't see over the pillows.

His hand drifted down her body with a feather light touch that sent chills reaching across her skin. His fingers traced the edges of her labia then swirled around her clit causing her to moan.

He reached over and grabbed what looked like a string of thick beads and ran it over her chest, never stopping his attention on her clit.

"Do you know what these are?"

"No, Master." Cami couldn't help but wiggle her hips, trying to get pressure where she needed it on her clit.

He gave her a sexy smirk. "Anal beads. For every orgasm you have without permission, I'll push another one inside you. And, slave?"

Her breath hitched at the thought. She had never even played with that part of her body. Was she able to handle this?

His finger dropped down from her clit and rimmed her rosette, sending strange jolts through her nerves.

"Yes, Master?"

"I don't plan to give you permission to come until I'm balls deep inside you."

He was an evil man. That's all she could think. She knew he wouldn't fuck her until she begged him. The snicks of a cap made her turn her head, and she watched as he coated the beads with lube.

"You already stole one orgasm let's see how many more you want."

He circled her clit in earnest now, and she fought against the orgasm that was building. The first bead was pressing against her entrance and she shook her head. He began flicking across her clit as he pressed it inside her. Pleasure washed over her as it breached her and as the orgasm racked her, she felt him pushing a second bead inside.

It was such an odd and intense sensation, nerves she had never known were there flared to life. Her pussy contracted, achingly empty.

His finger entered her cunt, while his thumb continued to work her clit. She thrashed trying to get away from the pleasure but he pressed up on some spot inside her and another orgasm crashed over the first. She screamed as he stroked over the magic spot and felt the third bead pressing into her. Sweat broke out across her body and her muscles trembled at the strange, overwhelming sensations.

"So fucking beautiful." His hands pulled away from her and the orgasm finally rolled to a stop. She panted and squirmed, tugging against her restraints, trying to get used to the strange fullness. "I think my slave likes having her ass played with."

Did she? It was all so new, she wasn't sure what to think.

Tek stroked his cock with slow motions, lust clearly displayed on all his features.

He bent over and nibbled on her over-sensitized nipples, and Cami knew she was almost at her limit for pleasure. When he gave a hard suck, she broke.

"Please, Master!"

She felt Tek's smile against her breast. "Please, what slave?"

"Fuck me." She arched up as if offering herself to him. The movement of the beads inside her almost starting another orgasm.

She watched with hunger as he put on a condom and placed his body on top of hers. With slow movements, he rubbed his cock over her clit in long strokes and she whimpered. He was so large she knew it was going to hurt, but no longer cared. She just needed him inside her.

He lifted himself and poised at her entrance, paused. She tugged at her restraints, almost feral with need.

"You're perfect."

She felt the stretch as he slowly entered her. The burn almost pleasant. He reached down and did something that caused the beads to start to vibrate, and another orgasm slammed through her as he thrust deep in the same moment.

The brief moment of pain was nothing compared to the ecstasy rolling through her. His thrusts were everything as he slammed into her, causing the orgasm to build higher.

"Fuck, Tek!" she screamed as he pulled the beads out.

"Cami!"

Stars flicked in front of her eyes as she came apart, not knowing if she could ever be put back together again.

Chapter 27

Be polite, be courteous, show professionalism and also have a plan to kill everyone in the room.

Tek stroked the purple hair of the angel blissed out and cuddled against him in the bed. He had never seen anyone so beautiful as they came apart. From what he could tell, she had been floating in subspace for almost twenty minutes. He had managed to get them cleaned up and some water into her, but he doubted she would remember any of it.

He had done kinky things before, even had a few women call him Sir, but when she had told him her fantasy, he'd about come in his pants like a teenager. The way she lost herself in the role was hot as hell and let him do the same. For a short period of time there was no outside pressure, just the two of them caught up in their own world. Her eyes fluttered open and her smile was precious.

"Hey, there." The rasp in her voice was sexy as hell.

"Hey, kitten. You back with me?" She wouldn't be up for more that night, but the silky feel of her skin against him was a temptation.

"Yeah. That was… intense."

"Everything you hoped for?" He brushed a lock of her purple hair away from her eyes.

She chuckled and snuggled into him. "Yes." She yawned. "Sorry. I know it's early, but you wiped me out."

They had both had a long day, but he had several things he still had to do before heading to bed. That didn't mean she shouldn't catch up on her rest. He ran a gentle hand up her back.

"You should sleep. If you're feeling okay, I've got some calls I need to take care of before I crash. But I'll be a room away if you need anything."

Conflicting desires tore at him. Making sure she was okay after the intense scene was top of the list. Sub-drop was unpredictable and he would have to watch her carefully in case she experienced the emotional low which sometimes followed a trip into subspace. But her safety was still in danger, and his company wasn't out of the woods yet. While he would love to spend the next few days doing nothing but learning every inch of her body, duty called.

Cami rolled so she was no longer snuggled on his chest and nuzzled into a pillow. "It's okay. I'm going to sleep a bit. Then I'll help you find Rick and whoever he is working with." Her last sentence was more of a yawn than actual talking.

Tek kissed her hair and ignored the ache in his chest as he got out of bed. He dressed, and enjoyed the sight of Cami tangled up in bed, her creamy skin a tempting contrast against his dark sheets. He thought she was asleep before he even left the room.

The sounds of someone in the kitchen startled him and Tek rounded the corner ready to rip the Prospect, who was supposed to be watching the house from outside, a new asshole. Instead he saw Max pulling beers out of the fridge, a grim look on his face.

Max slid a bottle across the island countertop towards him. Tek took it with his sense of dread growing as seconds passed and his usually calm and chatty Brother remained silent.

Max took a pull from his drink. "I'm too late, aren't I?"

"Too late for what?"

"To stop you from getting us anymore wrapped up with that girl." Max nodded towards where Cami was sleeping.

"Since when do you care who I fucking sleep with?" Tek took a long pull on his beer, trying to cool the anger building in his stomach.

"Since your dick could drag us into a world of shit, we don't need right now. Her problems have nothing to do with us." Max growled in obvious frustration. "I'm not saying don't keep her safe. Pay Kane's men to protect her, somewhere else."

"Let me get this straight. Dragon and Sharp's women needed help and you're all in, but since I've got money, I shouldn't bother the Brothers with my woman's problems." He was practically shouting but didn't care.

Tek had never before questioned any of his Brothers loyalty. Was it naïve to think they would be there for him? Did some of them resent the fact he had business outside the club?

"Oh, she's your woman now? Wasn't it last fucking night she was threatening Clean and the Club with exposure? How did you go from treating her like an enemy to fucking her in less than twenty-four hours?"

Had it really only been a day? So much had happened, Tek wasn't sure how things had changed so quickly. No matter how much he wanted to lash out, his Brother had a point. That didn't change the fact he wanted to keep her safe with men who were loyal to him for more than money.

"It's complicated and beside the point. Isn't it hypocritical that you didn't complain when Tari's problems got us in shit with the Bratva, or when saving Pixie put us in the crosshairs of the Mafia and Feds?"

"No. Tari's shit was Dark Sons' business from start to finish. Pixie was an innocent. Your woman is anything but."

"Fuck you." Tek clenched his fist around the bottle and held back the urge to throw it against the wall.

"Brother, you got your head so far up her pussy you can't even see what she is."

"And what am I, Jeffrey?" Cami's monotone voice came from the hallway behind Tek.

He turned to see her dressed in one of his t-shirts, the material loose and falling an inch above her knees. Her purple hair was mussed and the look on her face was not what he expected. Anger, hurt would have been understandable but the disinterested boredom was strange. Tek looked back and forth between his Brother and the woman he was coming to care for, there was a lot he was missing. Why did she call him Jeffrey? As far as he knew, Max's real name was Mark.

"I'm going to go," Max growled and stepped back.

"No." Tek stared at his Brother. "If there is something I need to know, say it."

Cami hugged herself as if she was cold. "I think he's a-afraid of me."

Max stopped moving, his chest heaved as if he was trying to drag in air. Tek couldn't understand what was going on, and it pissed him off.

"Why would he be afraid of you?"

"Because anyone who gets close to her ends up in jail or with their life ruined in some way," Max snapped. "Did she tell you her last boyfriend is currently serving 15 years, and she's the one who put him there?"

"I thought you said she goes after criminals and there was

never proof it was her. And because of that she couldn't be my hacker."

"She didn't bother hiding with him. Walked the evidence into the police and was scheduled to testify before he took a deal. We're not choir boys, Tek. Think she won't do the same thing to you?"

Tek's thoughts whirled. The Dark Sons MC had plenty of legitimate and semi-legitimate businesses, but they also ran guns, and provided protection for people who weren't even remotely legal. Would she feel it necessary to turn them in?

He had promised her trust and honesty. She had forgiven him once, and he didn't think she would do it again if he lashed out or assumed the worst.

"Angela." Tek waited a moment for their gazes to meet as he invoked their agreement. "Do you plan on turning on the Dark Sons or me?"

She curled in on herself, the robotic mask gone. Then she looked at Max. "When I was little, Mrs. Mardot was my N-nanny. She was the sweetest old lady you ever met. She had to keep working long after she should have retired b-because some asshole stole all her money."

Cami rubbed her hands up and down her arms and Tek wanted to comfort her but managed to stand still.

"She told me I needed to be smart so I wouldn't end up like her. I was twelve when I hacked the evidence to lock up the man who had hurt her. I felt like a s-superhero. So I kept doing that for others. My father knew what I was doing and while he was proud, he worried what would happen if I got caught. We came up with a p-plan." Her voice cracked.

Tek watched as she walked over, pulled a bottle of water out of the fridge, cracked it open, and took a sip.

Cami placed her drink onto the counter. "I didn't think it was necessary, but I found horrible things out about very powerful people who could be in a position to help me if I got caught." She nodded over at Max. "They came for me when I was s-sixteen. The first two days weren't bad some yelling, lots of questions, and isolating me without a lawyer or p-parent. I knew my father would be using the information I got to get me free."

"It is a simple yes or no question. He doesn't need story time." Max's voice was harsh. And Tek saw the man's whole body vibrated with tension.

"So you get to out what you think are my dirty secrets, Jeffrey, but I'm supposed to keep yours quiet."

"Max, my name is Max."

Cami looked at him with tears shimmering in her eyes. "For the next t-three days Agent Devin, Max, and another man called Tony kept me in a room so bright my eyes hurt. Th-they weren't supposed to give me food and b-barely gave me water. To end it, all I had to do was confess and agree to work for the government for the rest of my life."

Tek was horrified. He had been an interrogator for the military. Trained men on how to break subjects as well as how to hold out under questioning. The idea of a sixteen-year-old girl being subjugated to treatment that broke well-trained soldiers turned his stomach.

"I was following orders. I never laid a hand on you." Max's shoulders were hunched as if she had physically hit him.

"No, you were the good cop sneaking me bites of food and extra water. Trying to convince me to do what they wanted. I a-always wondered if that was real concern or if it was just another way to break me." Cami shook her head as if clearing away memories. "After my father got me out of there, I targeted people who abused the helpless in any way. Children, women, POWs, anyone trapped by someone more powerful, anyone who was helpless. So unless the Dark Sons prey on the helpless or swindle people out of money, they have nothing to fear from me."

"You weren't helpless." Max's words were hollow. Tek could tell he didn't believe in what he was saying.

Tears started falling down Cami's cheeks and Tek wrapped her up in a hug, feeling her body as it trembled against him.

"I believe you," he whispered into her hair.

It took a few minutes, but she seemed to calm and stepped away from him, facing Max.

"It took me four months to find out every d-detail of all your lives. Every secret, every mission, anything st-stored in the files of your doctors, teachers, family photos, and in the blackest government files. I could have d-destroyed you. Hell, I could have planted f-fake evidence or interfered with a mission and set you up for death."

Max leaned forward and clutched the edge of the marble countertop. "Why didn't you? You destroyed Devin's career, got Tony thrown into jail, where he was killed. Why didn't you do the same to me?"

"Devin was power hungry and believed the ends justified the means. Tony was a sociopath the government had given a free pass to rape and murder as long as he completed missions. You were a good man placed into impossible situations who did the best he could while also surviving. You did a good job faking your death. Even I bought it."

"Good to know." Max shook his head. "And the boyfriend you turned on?"

"We were never actually dating. He tried to seduce the awkward computer geek so I would help him increase his security on his servers. Didn't think I would look and see they were full of child pornography."

"My source didn't share that part of the story. I still think you're a risk." Max looked over to Tek, his face resolved.

"Dark Sons for life. I may not like it, but I'll back whatever you decide."

"Thanks, Brother." Tek reached out his arm and Max grabbed it pulling him into a back slapping hug.

"For what it's worth, yeah, I was supposed to be the good cop, but I wasn't supposed to give you anything unless you cracked. Seen bigger and tougher men crumble under a lot less pressure than you did." Max looked between the two of them. "Don't ever underestimate her."

Max left without another word. Tek pulled Cami into his arms. He wasn't sure why, but he knew she wasn't lying. She would be loyal to him and his Brothers.

"Joseph?" Her quiet tone reminded him that while he may be sure about them, she probably still had doubts.

Tek lifted her up onto the counter and stepped between her legs, putting them eye to eye. "Yeah?"

"You believe me right?"

He leaned in and kissed her forehead. "I do."

"You have to tell me if this is too much. My problems or any of it. I'm not going to change. I know secrets that could get a lot of people hurt, and while I'm careful, I've always known someday it would come back to haunt me. I just never had anyone that might get hurt with me."

"Don't worry about us, kitten. Me and my Brothers can handle it."

Chapter 28

"Find out who you are and do it on purpose."— *Dolly Parton*

For three days Cami spent all her time either on the computer or acting out horizontal fantasies with Tek. Her hands were cramping, and they were no closer to figuring out where Rick went or what the hacking group, R3publix, was planning or if they even were going to come after her again.

Tek was spending today helping clean up the digital mess back at his company, and she decided to take a walk to clear the cobwebs from her mind while some of her programs were running. Her current bodyguard, Grinder was giving her enough space she could almost pretend she was alone walking along the edge of the field.

"Well, look who finally came up for air from her marathon sex-a-thon." Heat crawled up Cami's cheeks as she looked over to the back of the house where they had held the bar-b-que.

Jojo stood in the doorway of an enclosed porch, Val and Pixie sitting behind her. Someone had obviously fetched her friend some of her own clothes because the drag queen was decked out in a cowgirl outfit that hugged her body like a second skin, a black bouffant wig done up in style on her head.

"Get your ass over here. It is time for some serious girl talk. Your gorgeous stalker can join these girls' stalkers inside."

Cami shook her head. "He's a bodyguard, not a stalker."

"If it walks like a duck, and quacks like a duck, it ain't a lion."

Cami jogged up and wrapped her friend in a hug. The last few days had been so focused she had forgotten about her friend and felt guilty about that. She had justified it to herself by saying her friend's skills were only in encryption, but that had been only part of it. Needing to find Rick had been her focus, and that meant moving at a speed her friend couldn't work at. Hopefully Jojo would understand after they both got back to what should be a normal life. The warm air inside the porch was a welcome change since she didn't really have clothes suited for long walks in the Colorado fall weather.

Pixie was sitting with her feet up on a cushioned wicker couch while Val sat next to her on another couch the whole enclosed porch was a perfect setup with a beautiful view of the field and the Rocky mountains in the distance while still being warm and sheltered from the cold.

"Good to see you finally out and about." Val's welcoming southern tone put Cami at ease.

"Hope you have been enjoying your time with Tek." Pixie smiled.

Cami felt her cheeks heating. The two of them had mostly been spending time side by side at different computers lost in code. Tek focusing on fixing the nightmare that was his security while she focused on tracking down the hacking group and searching for Rick. They had taken a few breaks.

"Looks like she enjoyed that time," Jojo teased. "So much that they couldn't even pop their heads out and say hi to friends and family."

Cami had totally forgotten she had been keeping Tek from Pixie. She plopped down on a chair. "I'm so sorry, Pixie. I didn't even think."

Her laugh was like tinkling bells. "Honestly, I'm still not sure I'm ready to wrap my head around having an older brother. Sharp took me in to get the DNA test, so we'll know for sure. I couldn't handle believing I have a brother, then finding out you were wrong."

There was no doubt in Cami's mind, but she understood the hesitation. It would be a big change.

Jojo sat down next to her with a dramatic sigh. "Yes, yes, you are about to become an heiress that is wonderful. But I want to know all the details of what my innocent flower has been doing all these long days."

"Innocent flower?" Pixie laughed. "Aren't you a stripper at Darklights? I mean I'm not knocking it, a girl needs to earn a living, but innocent isn't a word I'd use."

Jojo chuckled and proceeded to tell all her secrets to these two women who were brand new. From her being a virgin millionaire to her quest to find what she wanted sexually by stripping. Cami would have died from embarrassment if it was possible.

Val raised an eyebrow. "Your therapist told you to do this?"

"No. He said if I found myself uncomfortable in a s-situation, I should pretend to be someone else so I could get through it until I was comfortable again. Then I was taking a pole dancing exercise class and thought, I'm pretty good at this. One thing l-led to another, and it seemed to make sense. I mean, how else was I supposed to know what I would like?"

"Well." Pixie grinned. "I think most women meet a guy, connect, and give him a whirl."

"That seems inefficient." Actually, it was what she had done with Tek, so she was arguing against her own actions.

"My girl loves her data. She is probably going to have to try all flavors of the rainbow before she is sure of herself." Jojo reached over and squeezed her knee.

"Is that all Tek is to you? A flavor you're trying out?" Pixie looked concerned, and it bothered Cami.

Was she doing that? The heat between the two of them was off the charts and he was so smart she never felt like she was talking over his head, or he was just humoring her. She hadn't once worried about what happened next or if he would still be there, but the bubble they had been living in was likely to burst soon, and what then? Would he still want to deal with all her oddities after the pressure of being in danger passed? Or worse yet, would he try to use her like so many others did?

"I don't think so."

Val leaned forward, putting her elbows on her knees. "The men here fall hard and fast, and they don't let go. If you're not serious, Cami, you need to make sure he knows that."

"They only met a week ago. Don't you think that's a bit fast to be asking for commitment?" Jojo's expression told everyone she felt it was too fast.

"That's all it took for Sharp and me." Pixie rubbed her belly with a smile.

"Well, he must be a beast in bed if you agreed that fast." Jojo laughed.

Val smacked Jojo on the shoulder. "These two are a perfect match and like to show us at every opportunity. Their floor shows are legendary."

"Floor shows?" Cami was intrigued. Pixie looked like an innocent angel with her blonde hair and green eyes. Everything from the way she looked to how she dressed screamed innocent.

"Oh, don't let her Pixie style fool you. She loves having people watch her and Sharp fuck like bunnies at the Clubhouse. Her other nickname is Banshee, and she is a badass woman who knows how to take what she wants." Val winked at Pixie.

"Oh so we're pulling out the dirty talk then are we, Val?" Pixie's grin held an almost palpable mischief. "I may like putting on a show, but our Val here likes being tied up."

"Oh." Jojo clapped her hands in delight. "So Cami, what kinky games does Tek have up his sleeve?"

Cami thought over the last week and smiled. It was nice to have girlfriends to share this kind of thing with. She looked up at the ceiling and tried to remember everything. "Well, I like ropes, ties, and cuffs. Bondage in general. Edging is horrible and wonderful all at the same time. Knife play is scary but fun. Wax is enjoyable but really messy. We haven't tried electricity yet, but I have a great idea for a mad scientist and his creation that I thought we could try out, but that will have to wait till I can get the props. Naughty school girl spankings are amazing. If I had to pick, I guess my favorite is slave girl and master because we can work almost anything into that."

She looked down and giggled at the slack jawed look on the three women's faces. She bit her lip and wondered if she had over shared.

Jojo recovered first. "You've done all that in the last three days? When did y'all sleep?"

"We've mostly been w-working on finding Rick and cleaning up the mess at Tek's company. But doing ph-physical activity to break up mental fatigue is a well-known convention to increase productivity."

"You are more precious than a wiggling puppy." Val laughed. "So you would say roleplaying is your thing?"

"Yeah."

"How about PDA?" Pixie giggled.

Cami considered it. She had been taught public displays of affection were rude so never really thought about it. But if Val was talking about Pixie putting on floor shows, maybe it was different for them. Would she mind people watching while she did intimate things with Tek? There were plenty of fun ways it could work as either a show or a funishment.

"That's not rude?" she asked to be sure.

"Not on party nights. Actually it's kinda required to become an Old Lady." Pixie smiled, not embarrassed at all.

If Jojo's eyebrows rode any higher, they would have flown off her face. "I knew bikers were a kinky bunch, but public sex is a requirement?"

A bubble of joy flitted through Cami's stomach because for once she wasn't the one being shocked. Bonding over girl talk was something she had only ever done with Jojo, and it was nice to be connecting with these women.

"More a tradition than a requirement. Well, sort of. When a man asks you to be his Old Lady, the official ceremony has to be witnessed by at least five Brothers. The letter of the law says she has to 'show her devotion to her man and his club'. And tradition is you fuck claim each other in front of the club and vow yourself to the Dark Sons." Val winked at Pixie. "Some of us like to renew our vows on occasion, and others never do. That is a more personal preference."

"Oh Lordy." Jojo fanned herself. "So if my girl wants to join your little club and get one of those fancy vests she needs to get down and dirty with her man in front of witnesses?"

The idea excited her more than she wanted to admit. Not that he had even hinted he wanted that kind of relationship with her. Val and Pixie laughed and nodded, obviously enjoying Jojo's shock. The door to the house flew open and Dozer stood in the doorway, a grim expression on his face.

His gaze stopped on Cami and he took a deep breath.

"Sorry, ladies. Cami is going to have to come with me up to the Clubhouse."

Val looked at her husband with a frown forming on her face. "What's going on, baby?"

He ran a hand down his beard. "Cops are there with a warrant for her arrest."

Cami's chest tightened, and she had trouble getting breath. "What for?"

Chapter 29

I don't wanna work, I just want to bang my girl all day.

The code on the screen was the last thing Tek wanted to be focusing on. Sitting in the luxury of his corporate office felt wrong. The last three days had shown him what really mattered to him. Working side by side with Cami had been like waking up from a long, tedious dream. Her vibrant mind kept up with his in a strange mix of brilliance and debauchery. He loved how she could slip back and forth between working on finding Rick and kinky bedroom games without a pause.

The only reason he was in the office today was for the final inspection of the new code and to talk to the company lawyers. He had come to several decisions and needed to learn how hard they were going to be to implement. First, he had to face Lisen and discuss his plans with her and Kane.

His intercom buzzed, informing him they were here. Tek got up from his desk and moved over to the more casual seating area that held three comfortable chairs, hoping it might make this conversation a little less hard to swallow. What he wanted to do would be a huge risk for the company, and Lisen and Kane had been with him since the beginning.

Neither of them looked happy with him as they walked into the office. While Lisen's expression was almost hostile, Kane's look was more a mix of frustrated annoyance. He gestured for them to sit and took the third chair.

"I know we have a lot to discuss–" Tek started.

"You think?" Lisen's aggravated words cut him off. "The company is in the middle of a crisis, you commit sexual assault, armed gunmen attack, you vanish with your victim, refuse to answer phone calls, barely respond to email, and just show up three days later and demand our presence. I don't even know where to start unpacking this mess. If it wasn't for our long history and the hundreds of employees who would be affected, I'd leave you to clean it up by yourself."

"It wasn't sexual assault," Tek protested, though his words were hollow. He had crossed a line and was glad beyond belief Cami had forgiven him.

"Really?" Kane spoke up. "Lisen told me what you told her, and I watched the video of the interaction with the lawyers. Seems to me they couldn't blackmail you with a video or anything else if you had been a choir boy."

Both of them had points, but he didn't feel like getting into it with them. They had been more than coworkers and they deserved some information, so he decided to give them some truth. "Never been a choir boy. Cami has agreed to forgive me and the two of us are together now."

"Is that a joke?" Lisen raised an imperious eyebrow.

"No joke. Details of that are between her and me. The last week has brought home some very uncomfortable truths. You both know in the last five years this company has grown way beyond what I ever imagined. The original mission has become buried under the work needed to grow into corporate markets. Over seventy percent of our business now is in protecting the rich and powerful, both digitally and physically. I don't want to spend my time on that anymore."

Kane leaned back in his chair. "Not going to lie, most of the bodyguard work we do could be done by pretty muscle rather than trained military men, but the paycheck is good."

"Oh for the love of God, Tek. Is this some sort of early midlife crisis? I respect your goals or I wouldn't have stayed with you all this time, but the truth is you can't fund saving and protecting the helpless without the projects that actually pay." Lisen pinched the bridge of her nose. "Over the years, I've looked the other way on your business with the Dark Sons. Now, if you say you worked out things with Cami, fine, though I do want permission to do what it takes to get Joshua back."

"You got it."

"If you want me to continue to work for you, you need to be very clear about what your little statement means. This is your company, but it sounds like you want to ditch all the paying work. Not even your money will pay the salaries of all the people who depend on us for long." Some of Lisen's anger seemed to have been replaced with worry.

Tek understood her concerns and hoped they would both be interested in what he was offering. "Once we clean up the mess Rick made of the GUI, it is my intent to take a step back. Depending on what legal and contracts says I'm not sure how exactly it is going to take, but my intent is to step away and give the two of you full control of your divisions."

"It's not like we don't have full control now. You don't interfere much. How would this be different?" Kane looked puzzled.

"I'm breaking off the division that works on missing people and kidnappings into its own company. My plan is to run it personally as a private foundation, with a small team only subcontracting work out on an as needed basis."

Lisen narrowed her eyes. "Are you planning on selling Vallier Technologies?"

"In a manner of speaking. I'm giving each of you twenty-six percent of the company before the split with the option to buy me out over time at the current market value."

Kane coughed and Lisen looked as if she had been hit with a stick. The COO recovered first. "Tek, this is an over two-billion-dollar company and you are just going to give over half of it to us?"

"And all the associated headaches. If I were the two of you, I would separate the two sides of the house into their own companies, but luckily that won't be my decision." Tek leaned back with a smile. Even if it wasn't reality yet, the idea that soon he would be free of the day-to-day grind and free to focus on the important things in life was like a giant weight being lifted off his shoulders.

His personal worth was more than he could spend in several lifetimes, so giving this much of it to two people who had made most of it possible seemed right. His cellphone rang. Hawk's name flashed across the screen.

"Hey, Brother. Going to be a few hours before I can head back."

"I'm sorry, Tek. We had no warning." Hawk's voice was tight. Tek stood and strode towards the door, ignoring the curious looks of Kane and Lisen.

"What the fuck happened?"

Chapter 30

Doing the right thing has never gone so wrong.

The back of Agent Devin's car was surprisingly clean. Cami wasn't sure why she had expected dirt and trash, but the sedan looked like it might have been fresh off the sales lot. The gray interior was boring and other than the extra gadgets on the dash, you would never know. The car even had that slightly chemical smell that was usually only found in new cars. Her wrists chaffed under the cold metal of the handcuffs as they held her in an awkward position, propped forward against the seatbelt. She hadn't been violent or tried to escape, but for some reason Devin thought they were necessary.

The whole situation was surreal, from the walk to the Clubhouse, to listening to her rights being read. Honestly, her mind sort of checked out from the moment Dozer said she was accused of murder. Even as Deep, a man she'd never met, read the warrants, the only words that sunk into her mind was that there was evidence she had shot someone.

Having never fired a gun at another person, she found that impossible. In fact, it was almost two years since she had fired a gun at a range. How could they possibly have evidence otherwise? Faking digital records. Sure, she knew how to do that, but physical evidence? Wasn't that supposed to be impossible? She'd never really thought about the possibility.

Cami tilted her head and studied the man in the driver's seat. What in his past made Devin willing to terrorize a child whose only crime was wanting the truth about his father? Empathy of any sort seemed beyond him. When she'd gotten him removed from the NSA, she had been young and thought it would get him out of her life. Instead of being smart and moving on, Devin spent almost ten years trying to find ways to get her back under his thumb. Obsession might be part of it, possibly revenge, but the focused hatred he displayed was foreign to her. Maybe if she understood what he wanted, she could finally get him out of her life.

"What is the deal this time? Hack the C-Cartel's and you'll drop the fake m-murder charge? Or maybe you want me to tell the CIA or FBI I f-forgive you and am okay with you working with them again? Whatever it is, my answer will always be n-no. I d-don't work under duress."

"That only worked before because I couldn't prove what everyone knew you had done. This time I have fingerprints, the gun, and a dead body that says you either play ball or go to jail. I'm good with either solution."

Fingerprints… Gun... Her thoughts whirled, Tek's gun! He had let her hold it for comfort while she crawled out from under the car. Did he shoot someone with that gun? But wouldn't it then have both their fingerprints on it?

She looked out the window as her thoughts raced and saw they were driving way too fast through a small town. Houses and shops lined the street. The traffic was light, so Devin obviously thought he could ignore any posted speed limits. Behind them in a car was Deep and Sharp, while behind them Max and a Dark Son Brother named Highdive rode motorcycles. How had she gone from being on her own to having people she barely knew be willing to follow her to the police station? Her arrest wasn't a shock. She broke lots of laws. However, murder was not something she'd ever contemplated being charged with.

"You know what always confused m-me about you, Agent Devin?"

He snorted, looking back at her in the rearview mirror. "What's that, Ms. Turner?"

"That you never t-thought to j-just ask me to do something. It's like you only want my help if you are f-forcing or b-blackmailing me."

Within the small reflective surface, Cami saw Devin's eyes roll like a teenager. "Like I'm supposed to believe you would help."

"You'd be surprised. CA-million does work on request for the government a few times a year."

"So, you admit your CA-million."

Cami shook her head. "No."

The seatbelt jerked against Cami's chest. The screech of tires filled the inside of the car. She was thrown sideways. She barely caught the sight of the side of an SUV that filled the front window. Had it come from a cross-street? The view spun as the car turned in a tight circle and for a moment, she saw Deep and Sharp's faces before their two cars hit. Pain lanced through her and the world lost focus. The solid window bashed into the side of her head with a stomach-churning thud. She ended up on her side, unable to move while the car tumbled. The seat belt held her in place. Windows shattered around her.

When the motion finally stopped, they were right side up again. Devin was slumped over the airbag obviously hurt a lot worse than she was. Gunshots echoed outside, oddly muffled. She shook her head, trying to focus.

Hands jerked her upright. She screamed. A man reached through the window and pulled at her. With her hands cuffed behind her back, there was little she could do to stop the masked man who cut away her seatbelt. Tiny pricks of pain shot across her arm as he dragged her over broken glass through the window.

Outside of the car, the gunfire was loud. It came from in front and behind her. Cami struggled to break free. Her brain wouldn't focus. She needed to focus. Kick. Bite. Struggle. The self-defense lessons played across her mind. Unfortunately, the man who was carting her like a piece of luggage held her in such a way she couldn't reach any part of him with her mouth.

Behind them, the car the Dark Son's had been driving was a mangled wreck. Smoke billowed out of the hood and the front was crumpled to half its original size. She tried to find her new friends in the chaos. Deep was nowhere to be seen. Sharp was firing at her attackers from around the far side of the vehicle. Max was behind his motorcycle, off to the right, reloading his gun. She swung her head. Three unfamiliar SUVs filled the road with more men than she could count from her position.

It was hopeless. There were too many men with guns against what appeared to be only two Dark Son Brothers. They should retreat, save themselves. Cami didn't like the fear that racked her body. It was okay if she got hurt, but not others. Sharp had Pixie at home. He shouldn't risk himself for her.

Her kidnapper stumbled. Limping as if injured. She hoped he would drop her, but they were already at the door to an SUV. The floor of the car hit her already injured shoulders when he shoved her inside. She kicked out with her feet and thrashed with all her energy. Every movement felt like her arms were about to be ripped out of their sockets by the handcuffs. A large body from inside the car dove on top of her. The sting of a needle against her hip made terror shoot up her spine.

The world slowed and began to fade. Whatever they injected into her washed over her in a fiery wave. Her pain vanished in a rush. She giggled in relief before she felt consciousness slipping away. She smiled. It was good she had removed Tek and all his Brothers from her Dead Man's files a few days ago. Did these people understand how big of a beehive they had kicked over? In five days, some very powerful people would be pulling out all the stops to find her because in ten days their secrets would become public domain.

The room she woke up in smelled like old lady musk and stale potpourri. Her muscles ached like she had run a marathon, and sharp pain radiated from her shoulders with even small movements. Cami opened her eyes to see she was sitting at a desk in what might be considered a swanky home office. Her wrists were individually handcuffed to the arms of a big office chair. Packed bookshelves lined the walls. The solid mass of books was only broken up by a single picture window. By the only door in the large room stood a burly man with a gun in a shoulder holster.

The scattered furniture looked moderately expensive but was covered in a layer of dust. In front of her on an oak desk was a monitor, keyboard, and mouse that was probably fifteen years or older.

The man at the door noticed her moving and stepped out

of the room. Cami tried to stand but found her ankles had been tied to the back legs of the chair, forcing her to sit back down or risk tumbling forward.

The desk in front of her had drawers, but when she pulled on them, they stayed stubbornly shut. The computer was off, and she couldn't reach the power button with the small amount of movement the handcuffs allowed.

The door opened with a bang. She wasn't surprised to see Rick walk in with two goons at his back. Her old manager had dark circles under his eyes and his perfect hair was dirty and in need of a comb. He scowled at her as if she was an unexpected and unwelcome guest. She fought the urge to offer to leave.

The door swung open again almost immediately. The man who strode in was dressed in a suit that was obviously expensive and tailored to flatter his slender build. The black work tattoos that peeked out above his collar were an odd contrast to the expensive haircut and platinum Rolex watch. His cold eyes and confident stance told Cami this man was in charge.

"You were supposed to kill her, Ivan, not bring her here." Rick's confident, slick voice was gone. He now sounded more like a petulant teen.

The man in the suit smirked. "I wouldn't be giving orders or threatening her, Mr. Nelson, since she might be your only hope of getting the information we need."

"She's an intern who tripped over the wrong code. I don't need her help."

The man supposedly named Ivan walked over, and Cami felt her skin crawl as he studied her like an object he was interested in buying. When he brushed a hand over her hair, she could barely restrain a shudder.

"Is he right, Ms. Turner, are you just an intern?"

She doubted this man was as ignorant as he was playing. It wasn't that she thought she was some big super star people should recognize, more that the amount of effort that went into capturing her was too much for someone thought to be of low worth. However, giving him any information, he didn't already have would be stupid.

"I was w-working as an intern." Her stupid stutter always made her sound weak. But maybe it would be to her advantage here.

Ivan tapped her cheek with a light slap. "I asked if you were just an intern." He turned and glared at Rick. "Unlike your boss there, I do my homework. Angela Turner child prodigy, millionaire computer genius, and the answer to my current problems."

"W-what do you w-want?" Cami tried to hide her anger behind the all too real fear she felt. When the government had taken her, she had been young and confident they wouldn't kill her. With these men she had no illusions that even if she cooperated with whatever they wanted, they would keep her alive. The fact they were not hiding their identities meant they didn't fear her identifying them afterwards.

"Rick here made some promises my employers don't think he can deliver on."

"I need more time!" Rick protested.

Cami stayed silent. She knew whatever this man wanted, she wouldn't like.

Ivan's gaze was cold as he glared at her old boss. "Your other activities have brought too much attention. You have two days to get what you promised, or I will terminate your arrangement." His tone of voice left Cami with little doubt the man would be terminating Rick as well if he didn't deliver.

Rick sputtered and started pacing. "That's impossible. Without access to the Vallier computers, it will take me time to bypass the Dark Sons' security."

"That's why I brought you help." Ivan waved a hand toward her. "There are many people interested in getting their hands on Ms. Turner here, but I've put off selling her in the hope she can clean up the mess you made. Even I don't like the prospect of disappointing the people you made a deal with. I was hired to make sure you fulfilled your part of the bargain."

Cami felt like she was stuck in the middle of a spy movie. Hacking Vallier technologies made sense they had large corporate clients as well as ties to the government. Why anyone would want anything from the Dark Sons Motorcycle Club was beyond her. From her research, they dealt mostly in guns and protection. Their legitimate businesses would barely be of interest to anyone.

She had already hacked into their servers weeks ago when she took the job at Darklights. While she had looked at everything, she hadn't seen anything that would make this level of effort worthwhile. They had around a million dollars' worth of illegal weapons. They might be doing protection on something and the details were needed by this mysterious employer.

Too curious not to ask, Cami cleared her throat. "Why do you need to b-bypass Dark Sons' s-security?"

"None of your business," Rick snapped.

"I think she should know. Since she is probably your only hope of surviving the next three days. A few months ago, the Dark Sons stuck their noses into business they shouldn't have. To the surprise of everyone involved, they managed to take out one of the biggest information brokers in the world. Rumor is they got his files. Our employer wants that information."

Cami thought about what that could mean. If she had managed to get high value information, there would be no way she would store it on the same servers as she kept her other information on. Tek wasn't an idiot, and if they had something like that, he was the one who would've secured it. Finding something like that, if it were even available remotely, would be a long project and take more than breaking through a few firewalls.

However, if they wanted her to hack, then it meant they planned to give her access to a computer. Being able to contact the outside world meant she might find a way to get herself rescued. Alternatives started spinning through her mind so fast she was almost unable to keep up with them herself.

"A two-day timeline would be tight to break even mildly competent digital security." While focused on a puzzle, she rarely stuttered. "What are your resources and what is the hardware I will be working with?"

Ivan laughed. "Just like that, you are going to help us out?"

Cami cocked her head while she contemplated all the different ways she could figure out her location and get it to someone who could help. "If I don't help you, I get hurt or killed, correct?"

"You are very perceptive."

"You want me to steal information that was stolen in the first place." Cami hesitated in her thoughts. She needed to put up a token resistance or no-one would trust her. "I w-won't hurt innocent people, but other than that I am a reasonable p-person. I am n-not saying I can find what you are looking for, but I can try."

"I don't need help!" Cami didn't think anyone believed Rick's shouted words.

Ivan gestured to the computer monitor. "You best get started."

Cami looked at the monitor in horror, then at the ancient tower computer beside it. "You expect me to use that?"

"It's a computer what is the problem?"

"It is a computer the same way a kid's plastic beach toy is a shovel. Doesn't m-mean I want to dig out from a blizzard with it."

"She can't use my laptop. I won't be slowed down by her." Rick was a little too defensive, and Cami wondered what secrets she might find if she could go digging.

Ivan looked her over, then nodded and spoke to the silent goon across the room. "Get her whatever she needs." He grabbed her chin, forcing her to look up at him. "You may have value after this is over but not enough that I won't have my men kill you at the first sign you are double crossing us, understand?"

"Yes."

Chapter 31

Hell is not being able to kill the person who hurt the one you love… Yet.

Tek pulled into the Dark Sons' compound, his temper boiling like a kettle ready to explode. He had almost been at the station where the idiot DEA agent was taking Cami when he received the call from Hawk that changed everything. The crowd of Brothers waiting for him inside should have been comforting but his brain refused even that small peace. Yes, they would all try to help him find Cami not only for her sake but because the assholes who had kidnapped her were the reason Deep and Highdive were in the hospital.

He ignored the good-natured support he received as he pushed through the room to get to Hawk's office. All their support and willingness to fight would mean nothing if he couldn't figure out where to even look. Rick vanished off the face of the Earth. The Russian hacking group had no local presence. Tracking Cami was impossible.

Why hadn't he placed any trackers on Cami in the three days she had stayed at the compound? He specifically designed the safety system for Old Ladies to prevent things like this. Trackers in their phone, a piece of jewelry, and their cut kept them safe. But like an idiot, he hadn't bothered with Cami since she was supposed to be safe on the property.

Not that she knew he wanted to make her his Old Lady. Rushing seemed like a bad idea at the time. She probably thought he was using her as a pleasurable distraction. Hell, maybe she didn't want something serious. Neither of them had spoken about the future.

In his office, Hawk sat hunched over papers with Dozer, the Club's Treasurer. The looks on their faces didn't inspire comfort. The office was large with an oak desk and furniture. The walls and shelves held hundreds of pictures of the Brothers and the symbols of their military service. Usually this room comforted Tek, reminding him of the vast Brotherhood he was part of. Unfortunately, all his thoughts now focused on how much they had all fucked up.

"Here is what we know." Hawk in his usual style didn't bother with niceties. "Deep and Highdive are stable and should get out of the hospital today. Cheryl and Dragon are on sight trying to break free Sharp and Max from the authorities." Cheryl acting as a lawyer rather than rushing to the hospital to be with her Old Man, Deep was a surprise. "From what we've learned, they were attacked by men in three SUVs with fully automatic weapons. They flipped the car containing your woman and disabled our men's motorcycles and car. Then they extracted Cami while pinning everyone down with suppressive fire."

"She's alive?" Tek's chest felt tight. Surviving a car flip was not a guaranteed outcome.

"From what we got from Max before the cops locked him

down, he saw her fighting them as they hauled her away. From what you said, they want her alive for something."

The terror gripping his chest for the last hour lessened. So many things could have gone wrong during the extraction. If she was fighting, then she was probably still alive. His only lead, tracking Rick, was a dead-end so far, but maybe they could get more clues from this attack.

"I don't understand how that dick DEA agent got a warrant for her arrest in the first place. She should have been safe, locked down here." Tek paced, trying to work out some of the adrenaline flooding his system.

"I called our man at the local PD after the assholes left here." Dozer's voice held the same simmering anger Tek felt. "The guy you shot died in the hospital last night. Seems they got her prints off your gun. Agent Devin used that to push through a warrant, even though your statement clearly said you were the one to fire it."

"That is bullshit!" Tek wanted to hit something. The DEA agent deserved hell for everything he had done to Cami before, but the man had sealed his fate. When this was done, he would make it his mission to destroy the asshole.

"The case would have been torn apart before ever getting to court. Not our biggest problem right now." Hawk leaned back in his chair. "He's dead, caught a bullet during the fire-fight. Cops are holding our people till they can prove it wasn't friendly fire."

"Shit." Tek rubbed the bridge of his nose. The Dark Sons, who were at the scene, were good shots and trained regularly to keep up their marksmanship. If they had hit him, it wouldn't have been an accident. The investigation meant that four of the best of his Brothers were tied up while the LEOs figured that out.

Dozer nodded. "Found some interesting information about Agent Devin and the deal he planned to offer your girl. You were right to be worried. He had clearance to take her to a black site out of the country on the first plane available. Her first job was to hunt down a rogue DEA agent from Devin's unit."

Tek's stomach dropped. Could this whole thing have been a black op to get her out of the country? No one liked to talk about the dark things done in the name of country, but many of his Brothers knew the reality of how far some would go for the 'greater good'. His woman had already fallen victim to the gray morals of Uncle Sam once, and he was damned if they would get away with it twice.

"Was the attack an op or do they think it is the same crew that tried for her before?" An idea formed in Tek's thoughts.

Dozer nodded as if he also considered the double cross a possibility. "It's likely the same crew that attacked her before. Same weapons you described and professional tactics. Clean said internal actions were still in the planning stages and it is unlikely anyone was able to get two sets of mercenaries into town on such short notice."

Hawk leaned back in his chair. "We identified the mercenary group from the men they left behind. Once Clean and Max break free of the cops' questioning, we'll have them check with their contacts in the government. I don't think this was a sanctioned attack, but you never know with those idiots."

Tek paced, taking all the information in. "I'll work on hacking the mercs and see who is paying their bills. We'll know what they know by morning."

His President studied his face. The silence stretched and frustration bubbled in his stomach. He had better not try to stop him. Tek had all the respect in the world for his Brother and President but if the fucker tried to stop him, he didn't want to think about what he would do. Finally, Hawk nodded.

"All right. Anything you need."

Exhaustion and caffeine were battling inside his system. The clock on his computer said it was the middle of the night and the walls felt like they were closing in. His office was not designed for comfort. Set up more like a computer server room, shelves of computers and electronics lined the walls. The hours tracking the mercenaries from the moment they entered the country were well spent. He had their numbers and who exactly they were up against. What he hadn't figured out was who was funding them or why they were focused on Cami.

The door slammed open and Tek reached for a weapon. The files on his screen quickly forgotten. Jojo stood in the doorway, her neck corded, eyes wide, and fists clenched. Tek slid his hands back to the desk, not wanting to spook the obviously pissed off woman. It was hard to feel threatened when she was dressed in a costume-like cowgirl outfit, right down to a pair of sparkly cowboy boots that had to be a size eleven.

"This is all your fault!" she screeched. "You and your fucking Dark Sons' dirty business." She grabbed a box of cables and hurled it at him.

Tek dodged the flying object. His monitor wasn't as lucky and crashed to the floor. "What the fuck!"

Jojo reached for another box. To Tek's surprise, Max appeared behind her and grabbed her wrist before she could launch another missile. The two wrestled for a minute. Jojo might have some impressive skills for a civilian, but she was no match for his Brother. It took less than a minute for the hissing, struggling drag queen to be pinned face down to the floor. Tek shook his head. What the hell had sent Cami's best friend storming in here?

"Get off me! I'm going to kill you all for dragging my girl into your mess." Jojo tried to buck Max off, but the man settled his weight on her trapped arm and forced her back down.

Tek stepped around the desk, trying to find his calm. Jojo was Cami's friend. Helplessness was a frustrating emotion. How bad it must be for the woman to be left out of the search efforts completely. He would need to find some way for her to help. First, he would have to figure out what set her off and calm this situation down. He wanted to do that as quickly as possible so he could get back to trying to track the Mercenaries' money.

"Jojo, none of us realized what Rick was capable of. I get why you are mad at me, but that has nothing to do with my Brothers. Two of our Brothers are in the hospital. Injured while trying to protect her." He kept his voice low and calm, hoping it would help.

Jojo stilled, her wig tilted awkwardly. The ridiculous thing was about to fall off her head. "You really don't know, do you?"

"Know what?" Max's voice was strained, and Tek wondered how much strength it was taking to hold his captive down.

"Does the name Mitchell Thomas mean anything to you?"

Max let go of Jojo as if burned. It took Tek a few seconds to place the name. Mitchell Thomas was the alias of an evil bastard known as the Recluse. Human trafficking and information brokering was his specialty. He had kidnapped and tortured Pixie. Renewed rage burned across his skin as he remembered the horrors that man perpetrated on the world. What the hell did he have to do with this?

He was dead. The Dark Sons had raided his compounds almost eight months ago. According to his Brothers, his sister had beaten the man to death with a lamp. Looking at the tiny girl that was his sibling, it was hard to accept the brutal stories, but every man there swore they were true.

Jojo got to her feet and fixed her hair. The anger in her eyes said she was only a moment away from attacking again. She looked between the two of them and their confusion must have been apparent.

"At least you don't deny knowing the name."

"Start from the beginning. How do you know that name?" Tek asked.

She crossed her arms. "None of this made sense. Sure, you could make a pretty penny off of selling our customers' data. Insider trading is why corporations are willing to pay us so much. Identity theft is profitable but would have been caught too quickly. So I asked myself, how did Rick the Dick get contacts that were willing to not only pay him but kill and kidnap for him?"

Tek frowned. "The government contract we have..."

"Won't go live for months, and it's not like we have access to those servers yet. His cover is obviously blown, but these guys are still working with him. So I used the data Cami obtained from Rick's e-mail and traced the person he contacted back to their first contact ten months ago."

"What does this have to do with Thomas?" Max interrupted.

Max had a personal stake in that take down. When it was over, his Brother volunteered to help all the women they had rescued. He was still trying to track down and save Thomas' previous victims. Jojo had better be very careful with what she said next, or Tek might have to step between the two.

"At first Rick was asked if he had access to Dark Sons' servers. The idiot said yes. Over the next few months, he fed them every bit of data on our systems about this Club." Jojo made a gesture around the room.

Tek wasn't exactly worried about what might have gone out. The data kept on the Vallier servers was only for the legitimate businesses. He would need to make sure they changed any passwords or account numbers, but most of that was standard practice every few months. Since Tek was aware any system was eventually hackable, they didn't keep anything incriminating anywhere that could be tied back to the Club. Tek could see Max clenching his fists, probably imagining beating the information out of Jojo.

"Jojo get to the point."

"They got angry when he said he had given them everything. So he asked exactly what they wanted. He didn't get an answer via e-mail, but Rick keeps notes on his phone. His task reminder actually said 'Find the files the Dark Sons stole from Mitchell Thomas'. The notes gave a date to start looking from. The due date for the task was two weeks from now. I'm guessing that is why he got caught. He was trying to sell as much information to his other clients as possible because he needed to flee."

"How did we miss that?" Tek stood back behind his desk to his terminal. It wasn't that he didn't believe Jojo, but he needed to see the information himself.

"Unlike you, I spent the last few hours reading every single email in the file. His buyer switched accounts several times but always referred to Rick as Mister Nelson. Not M R but M I S T E R."

Guilt sunk like a lead weight in Tek's stomach. If this was true, it really was Dark Sons business that dragged Cami into this mess. Did her kidnappers even know who she was? If they only thought she was a mildly talented programmer, would they even keep her alive?

"If I hadn't gotten her the internship, she would still be safe. That girl is worth a thousand of y'all. Because I stuck my nose in. She has been abused and dragged into the muck of your dirty dealings. When we get her back, you and your Brothers stay far away from her."

Jojo's words were like knives sticking into Tek with every

syllable. Cami was a bright light in his life. What had he given her? He had done nothing but dim her brilliance time and again. She may have forgiven him for what he'd done before, but could she handle knowing that the entire thing was his fault? The majority of the information they'd gotten from Mitchell Thomas when they had raided the compounds had been sold to the US government. They still had copies, but none stored online. Even Max worked off an isolated system when he was tracking the girls.

Even if they saved her this time, would she be safe the next time someone wanted to get information on the Dark Sons? How did any of the men with Old Ladies deal with the fact that their women were constant targets for the enemies they collected over the years? Even his own sister was at risk. Could he live knowing the woman he loved was in constant danger? Pain lanced through his chest as he admitted to himself that he did love Cami and that no, he wouldn't be able to function knowing she was in constant danger.

"You don't know what you're talking about," Max growled. "Mitchell Thomas was human garbage who preyed on women. I'm sorry your friend got dragged into this, but stopping him was the best thing we ever did."

Max was right, and taking the man down had been right-eous, but they could have done a better job of covering their tracks. The government was like a leaky sieve and because they hadn't hidden where the information came from or the fact they had been the ones to do it somehow this mysterious buyer found out. That sloppy work had then put Cami directly in the line of fire.

His phone buzzed on the desk in front of him right before both Jojo's and Max's started pinging. The phones started cycling through alert sounds in an awful cacophony of noise. Tek picked up his phone and unlocked the screen. Displayed on the screen was a picture of Cami, a bruise yellowing her temple with the words *'SEND HELP'* written across the bottom. Text and e-mail notifications scrolled across the top of his screen.

Max and Jojo both flipped their phones to show they had the same picture. The sounds of footsteps echoed down the hall before the doorway to his office was filled with confused Brothers all with the same messages spamming their phones. His beautiful, brilliant hacker had found a way to contact every phone connected to their network and was making sure she was heard.

GPS coordinates followed in the next burst of messages. Hope filled his body with renewed energy. He looked up, ready to start organizing the rescue, and caught Jojo's gaze. Cami's friend was just as excited as the rest of them, but her words from just minutes ago dimmed his elation.

This was no life for the curious kitten he had come to love so quickly. They would rescue his woman, and then he would have to let her go.

Chapter 32

A real man doesn't need to make excuses. He can face his mistakes and take the consequences head on.

I t took all of Cami's willpower not to smile when she hit send on what she was going to lovingly call her Dark Virus. She still had trouble believing they'd retrieved her backup laptop out of her storage unit. She had thought it would take over a day to create the programs she needed on a new system. It was a pipe dream when she'd told them she already had a system set up if they were willing to get it out of her storage unit. They seemed relieved to have an easy solution that didn't require shopping. Her whole kit was delivered to her and the only thing removed was her utility knife. That meant she had a mobile hotspot and enough tech gear to fill a geek's wet dreams.

She petted the edge of her completely custom laptop and prayed everything she'd done was the right move. If she hadn't feared being put into 'protective custody' she might have contacted the police rather than the Dark Sons. Faith in other people was a scarce commodity in her life, and she hoped the Brothers wouldn't let her down. She calmed her nerves by creating hundreds of contingencies in case anything went wrong.

A light snore came from across the room. Most people looked innocent when asleep, but Rick looked ridiculous with a slack jaw and drool running down his chin. He was supposed to be watching over her, but other than a few disinterested peeks in the first hour, she'd been left alone. There was no way this man was a hacker. From what she saw on his laptop, he was more a corporate espionage guy. Not hacking, but sharing information he had legitimate access to. Hell, he was still using his Vallier Technologies laptop to log in.

When she'd asked him for the IP address of the Dark Sons' network, he had given her the address for the Vallier Technologies server. Thank God she already had the information she needed to get into the Compound's servers. Altering a program she already had, she was able to send out a broadcast to every phone connected to the Wi-Fi and broadcast her distress call. The GPS on her laptop said she was on a small farmhouse east of Denver and South of both the Vallier Technologies' Compound and Dark Sons' Compound. The one time they had let her out of the room to go to the bathroom she had seen several mercenaries in the front of the house, but in here it felt like it was just the two of them.

When the idiot had first fallen asleep, she had rushed to get the package together with all the information she had, fearing he might notice she wasn't banging her head against Vallier Technologies security like he was. That done, she had taken time to connect to his laptop and mirror it to her own since he had literally no security on the thing. From what she could tell, he had spent the last few days logging onto the

Vallier network using system administrator IDs and doing brute force searches of every directory he could find.

The search terms he used consisted of names and places that meant little to her, but she saved them for future reference. The door to the room swung open, and she hit the key that brought up a screen of code that was a piece of an encryption breaking program openly available to anyone who knew where to find it on the internet. Rick jerked upright and tried to pretend like he'd been hard at work rather than napping. The guard snorted and dropped a tray of food onto the table before leaving.

Cami got up, grateful her captors had uncuffed her after she pretended to be willing to cooperate.

"You should keep working," Rick grumbled.

"Like you were?" She was tired of his attitude. The man was as much a prisoner as she was, yet he pretended to have some sort of authority over her.

Rick rubbed his eyes, then took a deep breath. "If we don't find what they want, they are going to kill us."

"No, they are going to k-kill you. I don't know what they p-plan to do with me."

"Look, I'm sorry they dragged you into this."

Cami might almost believe his remorse. It might have been believable if she didn't know his request to get rid of her had started the whole mess. "I'm s-sure."

"If you hadn't poked your nose into things, I would be sipping a drink on a beach somewhere right now."

Cami glared at the man who even now was trying to blame her for his problems. "So it's my fault you can't deliver what you p-promised?"

"I don't even know what I'm looking for!" Rick practically shouted. "If the thing they wanted existed, I would have found it by now."

"You really think you are that good?" Cami couldn't keep the disbelief out of her voice.

"Yeah, I am. I've been pulling the wool over the mighty Joseph Vallier's eyes for over a year and no one would have noticed if I hadn't needed enough money to get out of the country. It wasn't supposed to happen this way. No one was supposed to get hurt, but then they offered me enough money to live the life I was supposed to have. How could I say no?"

He was a narcissistic child. Making over a hundred grand a year wasn't enough to satisfy his ego. It didn't matter the businesses he hurt by selling information as long as he got what he thought he deserved. One of the many things her father had done right in raising her was to make sure she understood the world didn't owe her anything. Too many people walked around every day believing that simply by existing they should get the best in life.

"No. It's a s-simple w-word. What you were doing w-was w-wrong." Cami wished she could find her anger, but he was so pathetic she couldn't dredge it up.

"Listen to you. You can't even talk right and you're lecturing me? Good and bad are concepts for the stupid, so I shouldn't be surprised you cling to them like a child to the concept of Santa Claus."

"Fuck you." There was her anger. How dare this asshole think she was naïve? She had survived hell. Seen the effects of evil on the innocent. The world might be made up of shades of gray, and the laws set up to protect the guilty more than the innocent, but she knew what was right and what was wrong. No entitled prick was going to convince her otherwise.

"You'll see, I'll get out of here. I'm just waiting for my chance."

"Chance for what? What are you going to d-do? Wait till I find what they need and take the c-credit like you did at work?"

"You don't know anything."

"I know you are a spineless w-weasel who p-probably used D-daddy's money for college and his connections to get a job. Other than deciding to become a c-criminal, have you ever made your own decisions? Stood on your own two feet?" Cami looked the pathetic man up and down. "You aren't a man, you're a s-spoiled child."

She sat back in her chair, not wanting to continue the pointless conversation. Anger and frustration bubbled in her stomach like the worst Mexican food. She focused back on her computer. Her heart skipped as she saw the brown square at the bottom of her screen. Someone was logged into the livestream she had set up. Was it Tek? She hoped with all of her soul it was.

The packets of information she'd broadcast gave them the information they needed to connect. They would get video and audio from her computer but not be able to talk to her. The risk of being found out if someone sent her a message at a bad time was too high. Her body shook with nerves as she continued to work on hacking the mercenaries' phones and connected emails for almost an hour. She checked the time. The Dark Sons' Compound was only about twenty minutes away. She knew they would have to plan and scout, but not knowing when they were going to rescue her was another kind of torture.

She let out a squeak when the door opened again. Rick gave her a dirty look. The urge to flip him off was a serious temptation, but she didn't want to risk pissing off their guard. One of their guards came in and bent over to pick up the now empty food tray, and her stomach dropped when she saw her nemesis stand with his laptop raised over his head. Shock held her still as he brought it down on the burly guard's head. Luck must have been on his side because the guard dropped to his knees, giving him the opportunity to hit him again.

What was this idiot thinking? Even if he managed to knock out the guard, there were plenty more in the house who wouldn't let him sneak up on them. A third strike either killed the guard or finally knocked him out. Rick reached down, pulling the gun from the holster at the man's side. He shot her a smug look and ran out of the room before she even really registered what he had done.

Gunfire echoed into the room. Cami dove to the floor, not wanting to risk getting hit by a stray bullet. The men she'd seen were carrying 9mm or 45ACP weapons, both of which could penetrate through at least five interior walls if they didn't hit a stud. She crawled into a corner, placing the multiple layers of oak wood between her and the location she assumed the firing was coming from. With the density of forty-five pounds per cubic foot, it should increase her ability to survive a stray bullet by significantly slowing its velocity.

A tub to hide in would be better, but that would require her to travel across the hall where she would risk being in the open line of fire. On the floor in front of her, the man Rick had hit still lay unconscious. His leg was only six feet from her with a small gun in his ankle holster. It looked to be a Glock 43. The boxy subcompact frame was easily recognizable. Should she grab it? Moving out of her corner increased the chances of getting shot, but having a weapon she could hide might exponentially increase her chances of survival later.

She crawled as fast as she could and grabbed the weapon and shoved it into her waistband. Cami scrambled back and pulled her shirt down to cover her hidden weapon. The mercenary on the floor moved slightly. She made herself small, trying to avoid his notice, and prayed he hadn't felt her stealing his gun. His groans grew louder. She realized that meant the shooting was probably over. She reached a tentative hand up and pulled her laptop onto her knees. The comforting brown square was still solid at the bottom of the screen.

It was like a virtual hug, but she wished Tek was there to give her a real one. How did she come to depend on him so quickly as a source of safety when things went crazy? Before, all she had were numbers and statistics, but they were a cold comfort. Knowing he was out there watching her gave her the strength to focus back on the room. She loved him, and that emotion would get her through anything.

She was tempted to tell him she loved him now, but a small voice in the back of her head stopped her. The first time she said I love you shouldn't be over video while being held hostage.

Chapter 33

Of the seven deadly sins, today I'm choosing Wrath.

Tek clutched his phone so hard it was a surprise it didn't shatter. It was almost three in the morning and he knew that all around the secluded farmhouse his Brothers were getting into position. The road leading up to the house where Cami was being held was well guarded. Several mercenaries were doing sweeps of the surrounding grounds. The plan was in place and although he had tried to run in when the shooting started, Sharp had tackled him and held him in place.

Rushing in when there were over twenty of the South African mercenaries guarding the place would only lead to placing his woman in greater danger. He stared down at his phone where the live video feed was playing. Watching her beautiful face as she rocked with the laptop in her arms was a kind of torture. The plan was solid. Once all his Brothers were in place, they would take out the sentries then close on the building. Tek and Smoke, their demolitions expert, would breach the window of the room she was in and extract her while the rest of the Brothers eliminated the threat inside the house.

Everything had been going smoothly. Then the idiot Rick decided to make his suicidal move. Tek ground his teeth as the view on the feed jostled and gave glimpses of her being pulled to her feet by a large guard. The computer was then placed on the desk. Tek could see a clear view of the room. He watched two men pull a third to his feet and drag him from the room.

"We need to go in soon," Tek growled under his breath.

Sharp gave his arm a squeeze. "I know this is hell, Brother, but we need to see what they are going to do."

"And while we sit out here with our thumbs up our asses, she could try something stupid like Rick and end up dead."

"Your woman is smarter than that." Sharp shook his head. "Fuck, she's smarter than you with this bullshit plan of yours."

"I don't want to hear it." And he didn't. The plan called for Sharp to take Cami safely back to the compound. The part Sharp and all his Brothers objected to was Tek planned to never see her again.

What he wanted to do was bust in there, drag her out, and claim her before all of his Brothers. She would bring endless variety to his life with her quick mind and body made for every one of his fantasies. Unfortunately, he couldn't have what he wanted. Jojo had been right. She would be safer if he left her alone. She wouldn't be completely free until they found the person behind hiring the mercenaries. Cutting ties now was the only choice, or he risked not being able to later.

"Yeah, well it's a dick move not giving her a choice, but if that is the way you want to play it I got your back."

Tek gave a tight nod. That was part of what it meant to be Brothers. You didn't have to agree with each other to back each other up.

Usually it was Tek's job to monitor communication and coordinate the teams through everyone's earpieces, but tonight there was no way he wasn't going to be in on the takedown. Instead, Dragon had his back and took over for him.

"I've got chatter on their comms." Dragon's voice came across the earpiece. "These assholes have three wounded, two shot and the third with head trauma. Picked up chatter from their coms, they are going to transport the wounded to another site for treatment."

"We go as soon as the vehicle is off site." Hawk's gruff tone was unmistakable.

It took almost fifteen minutes before a car pulled away from the house with five men in it. They were down to fifteen mercenaries. With almost double that number in Brothers, Tek felt his confidence grow. He had to believe they would get her out of this unharmed. Things had moved so fast between them it was hard to believe it was less than a week ago he had seen her dancing on stage in the little girl outfit.

The sound of Sharp's sniper rifle was his signal to move. He took out two roaming guards. Tek's team of five sprinted across the overgrown lawn towards the house. Deep used Det cord to surround the window but paused and gestured to the inside. Rooster, another member of his team, covered one side while he took position on the other.

Tek leaned over so he could get a look in the window. Cami sat with her back to the window, but she wasn't alone. A guard now stood in the doorway, standing watch over his woman.

"Fuck," Tek keyed his microphone. "Hostile in the room with the target."

"Roger that," Hawk replied. "Front will breach first. Five count and proceed with plan."

Tek didn't like the risk they were taking. These were trained men who wouldn't lose focus because of a few flash bang grenades, but there was no going back. Explosions rocked the front side of the house, followed by gunfire. Tek shielded his eyes as the wall next to him exploded inward in a shower of glass.

Tek entered the house through the newly created hole. He swept the room with his gun, trying to make sense of the scene in front of him. Cami stood pointing a gun in trembling hands at Tek and his Brothers. A man was bleeding on the floor, reaching for a weapon. Tek fired his gun, taking out the man before he could discharge it.

One of the mercenaries rushed in through the door, but his team ended the threat with several shots.

Tek almost didn't get his rifle out of the way before Cami barreled into his midsection, wrapping her arms around him. Her gun banged into his kidney, but he didn't care. For a moment he let himself enjoy the warmth of her body.

She could be his if he was selfish, but he had to let her go for her own good.

"I knew you would come. Even when I wasn't sure if it would be in time, I k-knew it. I wanted to tell you I loved you in case something happened, but thought that wouldn't be right over the video feed. I wasn't sure if it would be you watching or one of your Brothers and that would be too awkward to explain, so I waited. And here you are." She looked up at him with her expressive teal eyes filled with an emotion he didn't deserve. His heart winced. When she would finally learn the truth, when someone explained to her this whole mess was his fault, then she would understand why they couldn't be together. "I love you, Tek."

He shook his head, his throat tight with emotion. He had to let her go. "You deserve a better life."

Tek pulled away from Cami and pushed her a little too roughly towards Sharp. She stumbled, but he couldn't let her see it bothered him. He nodded to his Brother who laid a gentle hand on her shoulder. Another round of gunfire sounded from somewhere deeper in the house.

"Get her out of here." The words were dragged out from between his clenched teeth. The hurt in her eyes was almost too much to deal with. He turned and intended to clear the house with Smoke and Rooster.

"Joseph. Where the fuck are you going?" Cami's angry voice cut through the noise.

It would be so simple to ignore her and walk away, but they had made promises he wasn't willing to break. Hundreds of different responses came to mind, but there were hidden lies in each one of them. What he settled on was the simplest thing he could come up with.

"I'm going to do what is best for you. I'm going to protect you." He didn't look back, but he could almost feel her gaze.

"Why does that sound like a lie?"

"It's the only truth I have, Angela. Goodbye." Tek walked forward out of the room, ignoring Cami's shrieks as Sharp dragged her out of the house. He felt like an asshole and was glad when an enemy rounded the corner, and he was able to shoot him.

Unfortunately, there were no more men to kill. The echoes of 'Clear' filled his earpiece. He met up with Hawk and the rest of his Brothers in the living room of the old farmhouse. From the look of things there were no survivors, and his Brothers hadn't taken any casualties.

Hawk looked around the room, his gaze catching Tek's for a moment. "Gather up any electronics or personal items you find. Line up the bodies for Clean and his crew."

He received shoulder bumps from most of his Brothers and Tek tried to back down the anger that was starting to boil in his gut. She was safe. He was doing the right thing. The words tasted like hollow ashes against his tongue.

"Package safe and contained," Dragon's voice came across the coms like a final bell tolling the end of action.

Tek clenched his fists and slung his AR to his back. He would need to go away for a while. Make peace with his decision. But he couldn't do that till he finished the mess with his company and made sure everyone hunting Cami was dead.

Chapter 34

Life sucks, get a helmet – Denis Leary

Throwing any object that came to hand at anyone who entered the house might have been childish, but it helped vent the rage boiling deep inside Cami. Cutting up the sheets that still held the scent of their passion was arguably cathartic. Barely eating or sleeping between stints of computer hacking and crying was probably not healthy. However, the look of horror on Decaf's face as she built up a bonfire in the backyard with the contents of Tek's closet brought her the first sense of amusement in days. The fact she was feeding the fire with his clothes and expensive Scotch had the poor man frozen, as if he was unsure if he should stop her or stand by like the rest of her watch dogs had.

She sat in the bright autumn afternoon alternatively sipping the fiery liquid and feeding his clothing to the fire. Tired. She was so tired. Not physically, but emotionally spent.

Cami wasn't sure how many days had passed since the coward had ditched her, but it was time for her to get out of here. Everything reminded her of Tek, and since he was obviously not going to give her the respect of a conversation, it was time to remove herself from the unhealthy environment.

"Is it safe to approach, or are you still doing your impression of a major league pitcher?" Jojo's voice wasn't exactly welcome, but it was time to stop pushing everyone away.

Cami turned and saw Jojo wasn't alone. Pixie, Val, Tari, Cheryl, and several women she didn't recognize were walking around from the front of the house. All the women except Jojo wore the achingly familiar cuts of the Dark Sons' Old Ladies. Great, it must be an intervention. She wondered if they were here to kick her out.

"I'm done throwing things. I am at the burning his shit s-stage of grief. Grab a shirt and join me."

"Lord, child. You are a right mess." Val snatched a shirt and tossed it on the fire with a chuckle.

Every one of the women grabbed something and tossed it on the fire before pulling up chairs to join her around the fire. Their actions were comforting, even though they may not know exactly why she was doing it but because of the sisterhood, they would join her in her insanity. Jojo and Val set their chairs next to hers and the other women spread out around the warmth of the fire. Even though it was early afternoon, none of them seemed to think the idea of a bonfire was odd and most broke out beers and assorted drinks from coolers they had with them.

Conversations started and the quiet murmurs eased the last anger holding her strong facade in place. The warmth of her tears and the blurry sight of the fire were like a dam breaking and she sobbed for the loss of what should have been her happily ever after. Why did losing a relationship that had only lasted a week hurt her so badly?

ANN JENSEN

"Oh, honey," Jojo crooned, pulling Cami into her lap. "It's okay, you're safe. The men will find the people after you and then we can go back to a normal life."

Cami's body jerked in surprise. "That's not why I'm crying."

Jojo scowled at her. "Don't tell me those tears are for that snake of a man who got you into this mess."

"Jojo." Val turned her friend's name into a warning.

Cami pulled herself up to a standing position and crossed her arms. "I was in this p-position because a Russian h-hacking group offered two hundred and fifty thousand to kidnap me, not because of Tek."

"But they wouldn't have even had your name if it wasn't for him," Jojo huffed.

She loved her friend with everything in her heart, but it was time to give her a strong reality check. "Jojo since the government f-figured out who I was, almost ten y-years ago, not a single year has passed where some idiot didn't put a p-price on kidnapping me. Usually, I catch it before anyone comes after me, but things m-moved too fast this time. There have been six k-kidnapping attempts on me, four of them successful. Because of that, I have a kidnap and ransom insurance policy backed by a vicious mercenary group in Israel who are paid very well to make sure I come out of any situation alive using any method they choose. That is, if the US government doesn't r-rescue me first for fear of the secrets I'll leak. I've n-never let fear stop me from living my l-life."

Jojo looked like she had been slapped. All the women had gone quiet, their mouths open in shock.

"But you were so scared in the parking lot after the attempted attack," Jojo protested.

"It's not like t-that is something you get u-used to. Doesn't mean I let it ruin m-my life."

Val lifted an eyebrow. "So, it's not Tek that put you in danger?"

"No." Cami rolled her eyes, frustrated people thought because she wasn't physically intimidating, she was helpless. "In fact, as of this morning, I've t-taken care of all the parties involved. The Russians got the addresses of the R3publix hackers, and Mr. Ivan Ivankova, which by the way was n-not his real name, r-received a file with information of his that will be r-released to all of his enemies should I ever go missing for more than ten days. He a-assures me he has no interest in bothering me again."

Val chuckled and clapped her hands. Pixie and Tari seemed stunned and could only shake their heads. Cami grabbed the bottle of fifty-year-old scotch off the ground and took a swallow. She grabbed the remaining clothing from the ground and tossed them into the dancing flames.

"Why didn't you tell someone you had the whole thing under control?" Pixie scowled at the burning clothes.

Cami snorted. "Like they have shared any information with m-me? I'm just a h-helpless woman who has to be p-protected." The last words stuck in her throat as the memory of Tek saying them echoed in her mind.

The pregnant woman smiled, rubbing her belly. "Oh, how well we all know that song."

Laughter filled the backyard as all the women joined in with frustrated agreement. Jojo stood and pulled her into a hug.

"I think maybe my man bits might have led me astray. I'm sorry."

Cami rested her head on Jojo's shoulder and returned the hug. "What do you mean?"

Her friend stepped back and took a deep breath. "I was trying to protect you, I swear, but I may have convinced your man that if he loved you, he should let you go because you deserve a safe, normal life."

The grimace on the drag queen's face might have been cute if her words hadn't rekindled Cami's anger.

"I should be burning your Louboutin shoes along with his clothes."

Jojo gasped with such horror she choked.

Tari rubbed her hands together, a mischievous light in her dark eyes. "It seems what we have here, ladies, is a case of Alpha male martyrdom syndrome."

Cheryl cackled and put the back of her hand to her forehead in a dramatic gesture. "I, the alpha male, must save you, poor female, from the harshness of life by sacrificing my own happiness."

Pixie giggled, copying the pose. "No matter how much my manly rod wants to pound you into orgasmic bliss, I shall endure the dreaded blue balls because I know better than even your doctor."

Val joined the merriment. "Although your body can squeeze something the size of a watermelon out of a hole the size of a lemon, you are a frail being who should be treated like glass."

Decaf started choking and sputtered. "You ladies know I'm here, right?"

Pixie smirked. "Oh, we know you're there. I think hanging with the Old Ladies should be required hazing for every Prospect."

Decaf shook his head and moved further away towards the house.

"Do you love my brother?" Pixie asked. "And I mean accept all of this, his Brothers, and the rollercoaster that will be dealing every day with a terminally Alpha male who exists outside of the normal world?"

Cami almost wished there was a hesitation or doubt in her

thoughts after what he had put her through, but the honest truth was he was her perfect match. Their odd bits mixed into a perfect combo of crazy. Like pickles and peanut butter. Not for everyone, but oh, so good.

"Yeah. I want it all." Her whole body settled like she had finally stepped back onto the right path. "But I'm not going to chase after him either. I do have a little pride."

"Oh, I think I have the perfect solution to that." Val gestured to all the surrounding women. "Remember those lessons you were going to give me?"

"Yeah." Cami remembered promising to show the crazy southern woman some moves on the pole to entice her man.

"There are three stripper poles in the main Clubhouse area. I think some lessons are in order. I've never met an Alpha male who could resist staking his claim when his woman is putting on a show for other men."

Tari danced. "Val, you're a genius! I think tonight the Old Ladies should put on a show!"

Everyone around the fire burst into laughter, and Cami lit up.

Chapter 35

Telling a woman you know what is best for her is like lighting a can of Kerosine with dynamite.

Tek tried to let the cold air of the night cool his temper, but even with the autumn wind biting against his face he was still steaming mad. Riding his Fatboy usually was a calming experience, but knowing he was about to be on the same property as Cami had his body humming. The terse call from Hawk demanding his presence with no explanation had his jaw tight.

He still had nothing on the R3publix hackers or the middle-man whom she had described. Without taking them out of the picture, she had to stay at the compound. As long as she was there, the temptation to go to see her was almost painful. At least the search filled the hours that weren't taken up by turning over controlling interest of his company to Kane and Lisen. The gates to the compound were closed even though it was Friday night. His President showing he took the risk to Cami seriously.

After someone had kidnapped Tari right out of the Clubhouse, the Brothers had all agreed that any time they were on alert, the compound would be closed to outsiders. This would be the first weekend they would put that decision into effect. Party nights were how his Brothers decompressed and bonded. How long would they be willing to stay in lockdown for someone not family? He could offer to move her, but nowhere was as safe as here.

One of the Prospects opened the gate, and it surprised Tek to see Hawk and Max sitting alone outside in the chilly night air at one of the picnic tables drinking beer. If things were so critical he had to come in, what the fuck were the two of them doing?

But something must be wrong if they felt they had to catch him the minute he entered the compound. Last report had Cami sulking in his house and trashing his shit. He didn't care if she burned the place down. If it helped her move on, she could do anything she wanted. At least one of them needed to find closure. He pulled down the bandana he wore during cold weather and stepped off his bike, needing to find out why he had been summoned. The faster this conversation was over, the faster he could get back to ensuring Cami's safety.

"Reporting as ordered." Tek knew his tone bordered on complete disrespect but couldn't give a shit.

Hawk raised an eyebrow and took a sip of his beer. Max chuckled and shook his head. Tek grabbed a beer from the cooler at their feet and sat. His President wouldn't have made him ride all the way over here for a whim. Sniping at them would only make whatever this was take longer.

After a minute of silence, Hawk pulled a file off the bench next to him and tossed it across the table. Tek flipped it open. Inside were pictures of people getting arrested, along with several printouts of what looked to be Russian police reports. He flipped through the pictures, not recognizing anyone.

"Your woman's lost weight. I don't think she's been eating." Hawk's dry words grated across his nerves.

Tek's hand clenched and crushed the photo he was looking at. "She's not my woman."

Max snorted. "Then you're fine with another Brother picking up your leftovers?"

He didn't even remember lunging for Max but his Brother had anticipated the move and Tek stumbled forward barely catching his balance on the end of the table. "Cami's not leftovers. We protect her till she's safe, then she's gone."

Hawk tossed back the last of his beer and stood. "Then she's gone."

"What the fuck do you mean?"

His President nodded to the file. "All the R3publix Hackers are dead or in jail. The middle man Ivan is out of the picture. A team from I.M.C. will transport her to a new location tomorrow."

Tek took a step back and tried to make sense of the words. I.M.C. was a vicious group of mercenaries based out of Israel. Their reputation for brutal tactics and loyalty was well known. "Why the fuck did you contact I.M.C.?" His hands shook with the urge to lash out. This should have been his call. No decision should have been made about Cami without consulting him. "And how did you find the hackers?"

"You really still don't know shit about your woman, do you?" Max shook his head. "In between destroying your crap and drinking an impressive amount of scotch, she did all of that." Max gestured to the file. "And apparently she's had I.M.C. on retainer for over five years. She said the only reason she told us was so we wouldn't be surprised when they showed up tomorrow."

The world felt like it was tilting, and Tek sat on the bench rather than falling down. His hands settled on the file and he stared at it with renewed interest. Past the photos and police reports was her contract with I.M.C. Why did she spend ten thousand dollars a year to put them on retainer? There were even negotiated rates for different services, including the initiation of hostile actions.

Hawk stood at the head of the table with his arms crossed, looming as Tek read through the file twice. His brain seemed to resist letting the pieces fall into place. Could the picture he had built of Cami in his mind be that far off? A sheltered innocent wouldn't even know who the Israeli Mercenary Company was. He had known she had hacked and was on the government's radar, but this was a whole new level.

"Need to know if you are claiming that woman as yours." Hawk's voice interrupted his thoughts.

Was leaving her alone the right thing to do? He had thought he was keeping her safe by not getting her mixed up with the life he and his Brothers had chosen. If she was in so much danger she needed mercenaries on retainer, maybe it wasn't her safety at risk. He didn't care about the danger to himself.

The thumping of music from inside the Clubhouse distracted him. Hard rock and heavy metal was the norm, but this sounded more like what you would hear at a dance club in the city. What the hell kind of music were they playing?

"I like her for you." Max chuckled. "But if you aren't going to claim her, like right now, I think you better get on your bike and take off."

"What the fuck are you talking about?"

Hawk's serious face seemed to crack, then he was smiling way too wide for the conversation they were having. "Because, Brother, if you don't claim her tonight, I think there are at least ten Brothers inside who will fight you for the chance. Crazy is not my thing, but damn, if she isn't tempting."

Tek stood and pushed past his laughing Brothers to the door of the Clubhouse. He opened the door and finally recognized the song blasting out of the sound system as something by the Pussycat Dolls. The room was surprisingly full given the shut-down status. Almost all the Old Ladies were present, along with most of his Brothers. The nine women were dressed as if about to do a set on the stage of Darklights and right in the center of them was Cami in thigh-high black stiletto boots, a G-string, and a chain halter that bound her breasts in black satin and silver metal.

Much to everyone's delight, his woman was giving pole dancing lessons. Damn if the women weren't rocking the moves in their high heels and barely covered bodies. The sway of the silver chains completely captivated his attention, brushing across his woman's chest to the beat of the music.

Tek had seen plenty of women attempt to use the pole at the center of the bar, but none of them came close to the grace and raw sex appeal Cami displayed. It was like gravity didn't exist as she swirled around the metal, her legs almost cartwheeling in limber positions that sparked dark thoughts.

She brought her feet down to the ground over her head for a moment and Tek noticed across her ass, written in red, was the word *sweetbutt*. The growl that echoed up from his chest was audible even over the heavy beats of the music. The Club's sweetbutts were women willing to fuck any of his Brothers. Cami was making a statement. He prayed none of his Brothers would be dumb enough to take her up on the offer.

If she wanted to roleplay biker chick, he was the only man allowed to touch her. The Old Ladies had pulled up chairs and were inviting their men to sit. Cami was now spiraling upside-down by just one leg, her hands cupping her breasts. Her hair flowed around her in purple waves that gave glimpses of her gorgeous eyes that seemed heavy with passion.

The appreciative whistles of his Brothers grew as she moved into a split that had every inch of her skin not covered by the G-string on display. Tek didn't get off on public fucking like his Brother Sharp, but it didn't bother him. However, with the new revelation about his sister, things could get awkward. Actually, Pixie and Sharp were suspiciously absent.

Unable to let the show continue without staking his claim, Tek strode forward till he was right next to the pole. He had to dodge around the circle of lap dances as they turned into more than just innocent entertainment. Cami's smile as she stepped away from the pole was angry and feral.

She stuck out a hip, her chest boldly meeting his gaze in a way that challenged him. "What the fuck do you want, Tek?"

Tek held back his smile at her sassy words. Only when she was roleplaying or relaxed, did she lose her adorable stutter. If she wanted to play games, he was all in. He gripped her chin, running his thumb over her crimson painted lips. He pushed his finger into her mouth and pressed down on her tongue, forcing her tempting mouth open.

"You've got a smart mouth on you for a sweetbutt." He leaned in and bit the lobe of her ear. "I don't think you know your place. You are supposed to make a Brother happy. Do I need to fuck that mouth to keep it from making trouble?" He took his finger out of her mouth and dragged a damp trail down the front of her throat.

Cami snorted and flipped her hair, pulling her chin out of his grip. "I don't make t-trouble."

Tek ran a gentle hand down Cami's cheek and saw she was struggling to keep up with the tough act. He wasn't a fool. This show had been designed to push his buttons. It was his beautiful kitten's unique way of telling him exactly what she wanted.

He cupped her cheek. "And I don't mean to be an idiot, but that hasn't stopped me so far."

"What do you mean?"

"I keep forgetting to talk to you before I jump to conclusions. I should have asked if you wanted a normal safe life or if you wanted this." Tek gestured to the room where most of the room was watching as Deep spanked his wife with enthusiasm and the rest of the lap dances had progressed to a variety of fucking.

"Truth, Joseph. I w-want you. T-the good and the crazy. I'm n-not going to change, w-why would I want you t-to?"

Tek wrapped his hand in Cami's hair at the back of her neck and squeezed. "You want this, Angela? There is no going back if I claim you. You are mine and I am yours for life." He raised an eyebrow. "Did the Old Ladies tell you what was going to happen?"

Cami gave a small nod, pulling against his grip. He leaned in and spoke against her ear.

"Last chance. You say yes, and I'm going to fuck the sass out of my slutty sweetbutt. Claim her in front of all the Brothers here as my property."

Her gasp went straight to his dick. Her eyes sparkled.

"I don't think you can fuck the sass out of me, old man, but yes, I want to be yours."

Chapter 36

You may be a dumbass, but you're mine.

Chills and anticipation raced across Cami's skin at Tek's deep laugh. The plan the Old Ladies had come up with had seemed crazy to her, but she was glad it had worked. Pixie had agreed to stay with Jojo while operation Alpha Man Take Down was initiated.

She looked up into the eyes of the man she loved and shivered at his feral gaze. Her breath rushed out of her as he pulled her chest against his, pinning her against him with one arm wrapped around her body. The black satin of the bikini top she wore slid against her nipples when it was tugged away.

Without its support, the metal of the halter rolled against her skin with tiny pinches that sparked her desire.

"I want you to kneel, little slut and show my Brothers what perfect tits I'm claiming." Tek's words tumbled against her ear. "Roll those pretty nipples and make them hard for me."

He stepped back and Cami swayed, missing the heat of his

body. She was glad for her boots, the soft leather cushioning her knees from the hard floor. The gazes of Tek's Dark Sons Brothers sparked with lust that made her feel desired but not dirty.

As she began rolling her nipples through the chains of her top, she enjoyed the wild abandon with which the Old Ladies fucked their men around her. Tek circled her with slow steps, his protective presence making the entire experience a delicious thrill. Like being on a wild rollercoaster, you knew you were safe, but fear still thrilled your senses.

Tek stopped in front of her tsking. "I think my little slut is too distracted. Get on your hands and knees." He pulled the bandana off his neck.

Cami dropped into position. The cool floor pressed against her palms as the metal of her top brushed against her swinging breasts. The fabric of bandana Tek tied around her eyes smelled like him. When her sight was blocked, all of her other senses ticked up a notch. Music vibrated against her skin and the cherry of her lip balm danced across her tongue as she licked her dry lips.

Being on display without knowing who was watching was enticing. Fingers ran up her right thigh and she startled. The sting of a slap against her ass followed and she let out a moan as the heat of the blow shot right to her clit.

Tek peppered her bottom with firm strikes of his hand. Her ass came alive with the blows. Nerves sparked, and her excitement soaked the tiny G-string and leaked down her leg.

"Taunting me is not a good idea. Offering yourself up like this to my Brothers is not acceptable."

The next blow was harder, and her ass began to burn. She breathed through it and took the next one, knowing she deserved more than a playful spanking. After the tenth blow landed, she was glad for the blindfold as it absorbed her tears. Up and down her thighs and ass, the solid smacks landed until the pain merged into something more. It was like a cleansing of everything that had gone wrong between them.

She lost count long before he stopped, but when the rhythmic spanking turned into gentle strokes, her body hummed with anticipation. Her breasts felt heavy and needy. She needed Tek to claim her and give her the pleasure she knew only he could bring her.

Tek's breath was warm against her ear. "Now your ass is so red no one can read the lie you wrote across your naughty ass. You know I love punishing and playing with you but, I don't ever want to see you write something like that on yourself again. You are not a sweetbutt. You are mine and I don't share."

Pain zinged across her body as he slapped her pussy and she almost came. Her hair was pulled back with a wonderful swift jerk. She swayed, trying to get her balance as Tek used his grip to pull her hands off the ground.

"Did you hear me, kitten?" Tek growled in her ear as he steadied her with a collaring grip around her throat.

"Yes, Sir."

His grip tightened around her throat, not cutting off her air but with the promise of it if she dared to misbehave. His chest pressed against her back, and his jeans rubbed against the hot skin of her ass. She felt completely under his control and loved the rough, primal way he held her.

He pinched her nipples in a strange rhythm and it took her a moment to realize he was matching the drums of the music that had at some point switched over to something harder she didn't recognize. Tension built inside her, an orgasm starting in her core.

"I can hear your little pants. You don't get to orgasm unless I say so."

Cami could only whine as he pinched down hard on her nipple, the pain a wonderful jolt. She gritted her teeth, trying to push back the pleasure that followed. When his hand slid down her stomach, she whimpered and her hips jerked in anticipation. The jolt of sensation as her ass and nipples were abused almost pushed her over the edge.

Masculine chuckles that weren't Tek's reminded her they weren't alone. A woman's cry of pleasure and the rhythmic sounds of fucking caused her body to clench. She ached to be filled.

"Please, Tek." Her words were almost a whine.

His fingers slipped into her underwear and slid over her clit with firm pressure. "You're dripping for me, aren't you, kitten?"

His fingers slipped slowly inside her and barely eased the ache in her pussy. Needy sounds slipped past her lips as she pushed against him, trying to get him deeper. To her frustration, he pulled his hand away and chuckled.

"You get what I give you," Tek chided. "Open your mouth."

The feel of his fingers against her tongue was erotic. The earthy taste of her own excitement mixed with the cherry of her lip balm. She closed her lips and sucked, pretending his fingers were his cock. Desperate to do something to get him to move faster.

While she sucked, his other hand released her throat and slipped down her back. The rough jerk shocked her as her panties were ripped away from her body. The lack of sight made her feel off balance. When his other hand filled her in one quick thrust, she screamed her pleasure around his fingers.

He slipped his fingers out of her mouth with a chuckle. He was stretching her with two fingers in a brutal rhythm that was building pleasure into a tidal wave.

"Please, Tek, I need to come." Cami panted.

He slowed his speed. His thumb circled her ass, coating

the rosette with her own honey. New nerves sparked to life, and she didn't know how much longer she could hold off the orgasm.

"Who do you belong to, kitten?"

"You, Tek." She moaned pushing back against his hand seeking something to push her over the edge. She no longer cared if she got in trouble, she needed to come.

He bit her neck right at the shoulder and the pain pushed back her pleasure for a moment. Then it came rushing back as he twisted her nipple.

"I want everyone in the room to hear it. Say it louder." He fucked her with his fingers, rubbing along her G-spot with every fast thrust.

"You!" she shouted. "I belong to you!"

His thumb breached her ass as her body spasmed in release. He bit down again on her throat holding her still and the pain pushed the orgasm higher. She screamed her pleasure to the room.

The blindfold was yanked off her eyes as she started to come down. The bright light made it hard to focus, and she barely caught sight of the men watching before she was flipped onto her back. Tek's hand caught her head before it hit the hard floor.

His eyes almost glowed as he took her mouth in a possessive kiss that stole her breath away. The cool of the floor was a beautiful bliss against her punished backside and she groaned into his mouth. They paused, panting, breath mingling in a perfect moment. Then he was thrusting into her, the rough denim of his jeans rubbing against her thighs.

There was something dirty and delicious about the fact she was in nothing but boots and chains, and he was completely dressed with only his cock out and diving deep within her. He was claiming her in front of his Brothers, in an almost ritualistic way. She was wild and free in a way she had never experienced before. Knowing she would not only have Tek but this strange found family opened her heart in ways she'd never thought possible.

Tek arched up out of the kiss, grabbing her hips and thrust. Lights danced behind Cami's eyes as he just brushed against the end of her. She planted her heels onto the ground and arched to meet him in a rhythm that was undeniable.

"You're mine, Cami. My patch on your back. My Old Lady."

Orgasm burst over her as she shouted. "Yes, Tek. I'm yours!"

He slammed into her, his motions jerky. "Dark Sons for life!"

Cami saw flickers of light as the room echoed with the Brothers' answer.

"Dark Sons for Life."

Epilogue

Enter Thunderdome.

A few weeks later Tek sat at the bar in the partially full Dark Sons' Clubhouse waiting for Cami. They had moved into his house on the compound and often came over to join in the community dinners Pixie set out. His sister was ready to pop out his nephew any day now but still insisted on cooking dinner every weeknight.

This morning he had signed the papers that changed his life with a smile on his face. With that last piece of paperwork, Vallier Technologies was now officially closed. Lisen and Kane would separate, rebrand, and create their own visions from here on out with him as a very silent partner. Cami and he would start fresh and create a foundation to assist with kidnapped children and their families.

"Hey, handsome, come here often?"

Tek looked over at his woman with a chuckle. Cami was

dressed in red and blue booty shorts and a ripped t-shirt that said Daddy's Little Monster. Her hair was done up in pony-tails, but his favorite parts of the outfit were the titanium choker with a chameleon on the lock and the black leather cut with his name on the back.

He pulled her close and took her lips in a claiming kiss that had his dick hardening. "Is this where I tell you that you are my one and only madness?"

Cami winked. "Aww Puddin' you say the sweetest things."

"You two are crazy." Max sat at the other end of the bar with a laptop.

Cami snuggled her head against his shoulder. "You're just jealous."

Tek kissed the top of Cami's head, loving every unique thing about her. His woman had blossomed over the last few weeks. Her lack of stuttering was a sign of how comfortable in her own skin she had become. Cami's wardrobe was growing exponentially and looked more like something in a costume shop. Every outfit a unique signal to tell Tek what adventure she wanted to explore. He knew in his heart he would never be bored again.

Max did an exaggerated shudder. "Not at all. I have no interest in being tied down." He smiled and changed the subject. "Haven't seen your sidekick around lately."

"Jojo has been busy helping Lisen restructure their new Data Security company."

"Good for her."

Tek had let Cami's friend buy him out of a good portion of his stock after discussing it with Lisen. The two of them would be a force to be reckoned with once they got started. Cami stepped out of his arms and skipped over to study Max's screen.

"What are you working on?"

Max leaned back with a sigh. "I've been tracking the women we saved last year making sure they are getting the help they need."

"That's awesome! Why the long face?"

Max hit a few keys. "This one disappeared right after the rescue, and I can't find her anywhere. It's like an itch I can't scratch."

"Maybe she doesn't want to be found."

Tek knew which one of the girls Max was talking about. A picture of the statuesque woman with auburn hair had been sent to all the Brothers in case they saw her. Max hadn't even been able to find her original identity from the files they had stolen. Tek had run a basic facial search but found nothing.

"Or maybe she fell back into trouble. If I knew she'd built a new life or was safe somewhere, I could let it go. But until I know I can't give up." Max took a deep breath and gave Tek's woman a solemn look. "I've got too much to make up for. Mistakes I can't undo."

Cami placed her hand on Max's and squeezed. "You want some help?"

He smiled. "Tek already did his computer thing, but I appreciate the offer."

Cami giggled. "Don't tell my Old Man," she whispered loudly, "But while his hacking skills may rock, I'm much better at finding people."

Max laughed. "Well, in that case, I'd love some help."

A shout from the kitchen interrupted more discussion. "What do you mean you're having contractions!"

Tek was off his chair and sprinting to the kitchen before he processed the words.

"Calm down, Sharp. I'm not due for four weeks. These are probably just Braxton Hicks and will go away." Pixie talked through clenched teeth as she leaned against the prep counter.

"I can finish this up. If I'm still having them after dinner, then we can go to the hospital."

"The hell we're waiting, woman." Sharp looked over at Tek and the other Brothers now filling the doorway, his eyes wild. "We're going with plan Pappa 2."

Sharp had been creating emergency birth plans for the last month and sharing them with the Brothers via email and quizzing them at random times. The plans had ranged from what to do in a blizzard, or natural disaster to the more normal. Tek smiled at how twisted up the usual calm man was.

Tek watched as Hawk took off at a jog out the back door. He was headed to the chopper that Tek had parked there two weeks ago to help reduce his Brother's stress over the distance needed to travel. Cami slipped by him to stand next to his sister. She rubbed Pixies back while his other Brothers started calling for Doc.

"What is Pappa 2?" Pixie stood, her breath returning to normal.

Tek smiled as Sharp ran to the pantry, probably to grab one of the hundreds of go bags he had stashed around the compound. "You, Sharp, and Doc get a helicopter ride to Denver Health."

Tek used his phone to send the message to the hospital so they would be ready, and the flight path cleared. Even if it was a false alarm, it was best to be prepared. It was amazing what you could get arranged with money. The costs and the headache involved in arranging things had been his gift to the parents to be.

"I was wondering why that thing was p-parked in the m-middle of the compound." Cami was trying but failing to hide her amusement.

"No! Absolutely not! The lasagna will be done in ten

minutes. Then we can take the car in if you insist." Pixie stomped her foot as if that would affect her stubborn man.

"We are doing this, Darlin'. Stop arguing." Sharp's voice echoed with command.

Pixie looked ready to do battle, but Cami's hand on her arm stopped whatever she was going to say.

"I've got the lasagna. You should just give in. Helicopter rides are fun."

Pixie stomped her foot again, but whatever she was going to say was lost in her grunt of pain. A splashing noise startled them all, and Tek looked down to see a small puddle forming under his sister.

Doc pushed his way into the room and Tek barely registered anything that went on after that. Pixie's water had broken! He was about to become an uncle. His sister was a lunatic. Shouting instructions for the lasagna as Sharp carried her out the door.

Six hours later, Tek stood with Cami at his side in Pixie's hospital room. His sister looked tired, but her happiness was something that filled the air like the warmth of a fire. Val, Dozer, and Hawk stood at the foot of the bed—all of them admiring the tiny miracle in his sister's arms.

Pixie looked up at Sharp and smiled. She ran a finger down the baby's cheek. "I would like you all to meet Sean Joseph Oliver. Named after his father and his uncle—two of the strongest men I know. All of you are the family I always dreamed of. Thank you for giving me a home."

The world felt like it got a little bit brighter. Tek hugged Cami to his side and marveled at how after so many years of struggling he was finally completely happy. He gave Sharp a nod and shared a look with his Brothers. This is what they all fought for. This was the life they would defend with the last breath in their bodies.

Val cleared her throat and rubbed her very pregnant belly.

"Don't you fuss, girl. You and that baby are family. Remember. Dark Sons for life."

They all chuckled and smiled.

"Dark Sons for life."

The End

Ann Jensen

I'm a snarky Jersey Woman who dreamed of one day becoming an Author. I write Romance with bigger than life characters who have to dodge every obstacle I gleefully throw in their paths. Somehow my characters also find time for steamy fun on their way to their HEAs.

I'm an avid reader, engineer, photographer, and a proud Bi woman. My life is a journey that I hope never stops in one place too long. I fill it with love and laughter whenever possible and when I can't, I pull out my clue by four and use it with deadly precision.

https://annjensenwrites.com/

Dark Sons Motorcycle Club
Saved by the Dark
Lost in the Dark
Caught in the Dark

Blushing Books

Blushing Books is the oldest eBook publisher on the web. We've been running websites that publish steamy romance and erotica since 1999, and we have been selling eBooks since 2003. We have free and promotional offerings that change weekly, so please do visit us at http://www.blushingbooks.com/free.

Blushing Books Newsletter

Please join the Blushing Books newsletter
to receive updates & special promotional offers.
You can also join by using your mobile phone:
Just text BLUSHING to 22828.

Every month, one new sign up via text messaging will receive
a $25.00 Amazon gift card, so sign up today!

Made in the USA
Columbia, SC
03 November 2021